One Second Per Second

One Second Per Second

S. D. UNWIN

For Heather, Stephen and Gareth.

ONE

I swerve a tumbleweed the size of a Mini Cooper. They just come at you one after another, one with another. It's not possible to dodge them all so some you just have to take head-on, let them roll over you and make them a problem for the guy behind. Growing up I couldn't wait to get out of this place. And now I'm back. Physics was my ticket out. In a way, I left town with the circus because many of my heroes, the men and women who had ignited my love of science, now seem quite clownish in hindsight. Even my greatest hero, Albert Einstein, had been wrong in so many important ways—ways that have shriveled my confidence in any understanding of things. *Time is the fourth dimension. Nothing travels faster than the speed of light.* All the profound insights that put my dear Albert at the top of the physics heap now turn out to be BS. And though physics got me out of this place, it also brought me back.

I show my pass at the site gate, drive across five miles of southeastern Washington state desert then park in the TMA lot. That's the Time Management Agency. Clever name. They figured that if the agency's name was ever mentioned indiscreetly then it'd be assumed its mission is work efficiency. You know: how to plan your day or politely end a Zoom call. The TMA Building stands center among half a dozen smaller structures. Not a lot of architectural detail was lavished on these buildings that look like trailers grown up without supervision. More metal than glass or brick, and usually shrouded in a shimmer of brutal desert heat.

I brace myself. I had left at least three arguments on simmer last night and will be required to pick them up where I had left off. I just had to decide in which order I'd take them on. Argument 1: I say it's better to reverse Protocols #1 and #2 because that'd accelerate Phase A outcomes. On reflection, I was wrong. I'll save that one until last because my being wrong makes my opponent no less of an asshole. Argument #2: This one relates to an arcane point of quantum field theory and about which only I and my opponent care. Finally, Argument #3: I cannot remember what it was but I was animated and rude. Someone will remind me.

Kasper Asmus. Is he really going to be my first conversation of the day? Kasper has the mantle of most arrogant little shit on campus, and he's up against some pretty stiff competition.

"Did you read my paper?" he asks as a *good morning.*

"No, sorry, not yet," I reply looking toward the kitchen where coffee will be found. His incredulity is unconcealed. "That it?" I ask, noticing the stapled sheets in his hand. "Let me look now." That'll peeve him—me taking just a cursory glance outside the snack room when I was supposed to dedicate a full evening to it. I read. "What is this?" He stares at me, then swivels to look.

"What do you mean?"

"This notation. What is it?" He sees the problem and smiles smugly.

"That's my block mathematical notation," he says.

"Is it? I see. You've developed your own notation."

"Yes, it's better—succinct." I don't look up.

"So I don't only have to understand your idea, but have to learn your invented notation first?" No answer, so I look at him. He's satisfyingly discomfited. "Did you consider cuneiform?" He stares stupidly. "You know, instead of English. That'd really slow us up." I put the paper back into his hand and walk toward the coffee.

I don't know why I have to be like this. He's a young guy full of ideas yet I get satisfaction in beating him down. Was I always this way? He's brilliant and maybe his new notation will be universal in ten years, but I just can't get past not liking him. I should be nurturing him. Am I the asshole? Isaac Newton was an asshole—jealous, suspicious, conniving. Maybe it goes with the territory. Like I'm in Newton's territory. But then Einstein was a nice guy, wasn't he? No, I can't be an asshole. No asshole worries about being an asshole.

The hot, black coffee hits the spot and I navigate cubicles toward the control room. No one nurtures anyone here. Why is that? And it only seems to get worse. Is it to do with everyone being very smart? Maybe it *does* go with the territory. Before I came to TMA I'd worked in friendly, collegial environments where everyone was respected and had a voice—everyone was valued and contributed through civil discourse and compromise. And in those places I would have been hard-pressed to find a single first-rate mind. If true, it's a depressing correlation.

I enter the control room and see Jenn is in the Big Chair. Half a dozen others are scattered around consoles and facing a wall screen displaying a projection of the Earth's surface. Maybe two dozen red lights pinpoint locations on the map with a caption below each: University of Maryland, College Park; Delphi Pharmaceuticals, Edinburgh UK; University of Mumbai, India ...

"Quiet night?" I ask Jenn.

"Not especially," she replies.

"Correlations?" I ask.

"No," she says. That's always a relief. It means the incidents are probably not a concerted effort and are no more than random events across the globe.

3

A green light illuminates in South Korea. "Yonsei University. Twelve seconds per second". That's a moderate forward rate, but I've come to understand that time is fragile and what seems like a small time acceleration can be catastrophic with the potential for lives lost, futures vanished, and civilizations buried before they see the light of day. It's unfathomable to me that nature puts no safeguards in place to prevent this sort of thing. So it's left to us to deal with it: a handful of arrogant jackasses in a few tin buildings in the middle of nowhere.

All eyes are on the map. "Confirm echo?" Joe Alvarez asks without looking back.

"Affirmative to echo," Jenn says. Here I'm used to feeling nothing. You'd expect at least a tremor, a rumble or a crack of lightning given the scale of what just happened, but no. Nothing. The only evidence of something having happened is that the green light in Korea turns red.

"Completed," Alvarez says.

"Completed confirmed," someone calls. Another disaster averted. We get about a dozen of these a day. Zero on a good day, twenty on a bad one. But we deal with each of them. One second per second is how it should be and we do our job making sure that that's what happens, always, everywhere. For a team that barely knows what we're doing, we do pretty well. So that one's over for us, but in the other Washington the paperwork is just gearing-up. There will be investigations, government-to-government dialogs, voluminous findings, and action plans.

Jenn is staring at that new red light to make sure it stays red. It's never routine and that's not a chair I want to sit in. I look back through the glass wall of the control room and Kasper Asmus has his nose up against it. Now *there's* someone who does want to sit in that chair. We lock eyes and he blinks first.

4

TWO

The greatest scientific challenge of our age had never been to invent a machine that enables time travel; it was to invent one that prevents it.

Some think that the universe was designed. If it was, I'm guessing that whoever did that job doesn't include it on their resume. It'd be too much of an embarrassment, and so they'd have a 14 billion year gap that would need to be explained at their next job interview. That the universe is indifferent and disinterested is a truth with which most of us are reconciled. But we had thought that at least the world made some sense—that what we see and experience is some rough approximation of the way the universe actually is. How could my heroes have had any way of knowing how untrue that is? Of knowing that nature's most basic building block, its most fundamental ingredient—time itself—is in reality a bit of an imbecile and in dire need of adult supervision. What I do is manage time.

One second per second is the perfect pace for time. It's dead center of the Goldilocks zone—just right and not open to improvement. It was good enough to evolve life on Earth; just fine to produce great ideas like democracy, human rights and cheese, and even a universe of galaxies,

5

stars and worlds came into being at that comfortable pace. It all happened at one second per second. Fifty years per second hurtling into the future, or negative millennia per second plummeting into the past are the stuff of chaos. And yet the universe, it turns out, is just fine with it and its consequences. Time travel, once figured out, is embarrassingly easy. Nature puts no barriers to it in place, and even makes it hard to avoid. If there is any kind of cosmic plan, it's one in which time is chaos, and people, civilizations and realities its playthings. My day job is to confound that plan.

THREE

There may be tumbleweed but there are also grapes. I drive by uncountable rows of neatly-trained vines into a Red Mountain sunset. The Dog Star Winery is a modest garage-like box compared to the faux-chateaux structures further up the vine-covered slope. Its parking lot is crowded with cars and guests who have overflowed from the tasting room. The Release Party for the newest Dog Star Cabernet is an invitation-only affair and I recognize some of the revelers that I circumnavigate or push through to get to the winery entrance. Inside, guests have formed huddles and as always, the biggest huddle is centered on Bess. I grab a glass of red from the bar and look around for someone I might know. I'm not one for breaking into an ongoing conversation so I wait and sip.

Bess always told me you need two things to be a successful winemaker. Making okay wine is one of them but the second one is more important. It's having a good backstory. Bess's business partner has the okay wine covered but Bess is the one with the backstory. Astrophysicist turned winemaker: eyes lowered from the heavens to the earth. Nonsense of course, but how many other wineries can claim an astrophysicist? Bess sees me and breaks out from her huddle of admirers.

"I know, sorry," I say quickly. I'm late.

"Fuck, Joad. I've got eighty people milling around, getting drunk and wondering if there really is a new release," she says smiling, but not for me.

"You didn't have to–" I begin, then her face creases into a yet wider smile as a passing admirer puts a hand on her arm.

"None of this matters to you, I know–"

"It *does* matter," I say. She shakes her head, smile still intact. "I don't have a job where I can just take off an apron and head home."

"I know. You have a very important job, Joad." *Unlike me* is left unsaid and the smile slips.

"This? Now?" However she was about to reply, and her big, brown, crazed eyes foreshadowed something savage, it is put on hold as her business partner calls her over. I nod a thankful greeting at him. In fairness, the treatment I can look forward to is deserved because Bess had reminded me not to be late at least three times over breakfast. I return to the bar for a second glass. Den, the partner, is Byronic with heavy, overly-tended eyebrows which alone announce a supercilious arrogance. He and Bess are well-coordinated. Black hair hanging straight from a middle parting, his a clip shorter than hers, loose white open-neck shirts and infeasibly tight black jeans. Like twins. Incestuous twins (I'm almost certain). He puts his arm around Bess and leads her out to the barrel cave. It's not really a cave because garages, as a rule, are not attached to caves. At some point, and I don't know exactly when, Den became the type of person Bess admires.

After a few minutes they emerge from the cave and Den helps Bess up onto the bar.

"Welcome," she says softly but it commands the attention of the room. "I'm excited." She laughs and someone whoops. Winery staff circulate with trays of red wine and I grab a glass. This is the launch of the 2018 vintage which has been three years in the making. I do a mental calculation. Yesterday's Vancouver event could have taken someone back to that harvest in a third of a second. That was a bad event by any standard, the kind that turns your flesh cold. Negative 315 million seconds per second. At that acceleration, it'd take four minutes to get back to the founding of the Roman republic. And the further back some hapless wanderer travels, exponentially greater is the potential for disaster. At least that's the theory.

Bess knows nothing about my job, but at least she knows she knows nothing. My story to her is only a half-lie, yet still distant from truth. She stopped asking of course, but where there's dishonesty between a couple, it can be tough to limit. As far as Bess and anyone else who asks is concerned, I work on an academic project to detect exotic fundamental particles. And that's almost true. Just how exotic those particles are, and why I do it–those are the things within the wall of secrecy.

The particles are called tachyons. It turns out that when nature sits back and looks on gormlessly as time acceleration occurs, then these tachyons are emitted and at TMA we're in the business of detecting them. Tachyons are the strangest little buggers but thank god they exist, because without them, and without our pinpointing where they came from, we'd be in a world of incoherence and chaos.

And when I say they're exotic, I understate it. While the speed of light is the upper limit for all other things, for tachyons it's the lower speed limit. That's as slow as they can go. Einstein thought that nothing could travel faster than light, but these mad little things shoot through Einstein's grave at warp speed.

"I love the color–it's a deep ruby isn't it?" Bess has started the tasting of the new Dog Star release and is holding her glass up to the fluorescent light. "There's the usual blackcurrant, but do you get the herbal notes? Lavender? Some licorice, too?" There's excited affirmation of her analysis, verging on the sycophantic. Den nods approvingly.

He's the one who makes this booze but she's the one who sells it. I really don't get any herbs at all.

We're surrounded by twenty acres of Dog Star vineyards, lovingly tended and surgically harvested. Thirty miles north of here, buried below a shanty town of overgrown trailers is a 700-acre tachyon detection array. It sits silently, stirring only to send an electrical signal that illuminates a green light on a map half a mile above when a tachyon source is detected, triangulated, pinpointed, and analyzed. Then, when the director–the one in the Big Chair– so decides, the tachyon beam is reflected, phase-shifted, amplified, and beamed back to whence it came, destructively interfering with the source emission. This seems to do the trick. We're not a hundred percent sure why, but the temporal acceleration is arrested and we're saved. Saved from what is something we're not entirely sure about. I'm comforted in my ignorance by the fact that throughout history, many inventions seemed to have worked long before anyone knew why. How long did it take after the invention of the transistor for a real understanding of semiconductors? I can't remember because the Cabernet is kicking-in. Of course, at stake with transistors was tinny music and not the very fabric of space and time.

I think I do taste the lavender now but I reach for a second glass to be sure. Hearing my name yanks me out of my muddled thoughts. Bess is reaching for me from her elevated position and her audience is looking back at me, happy to be involved. I walk through the parting throng to hold Bess's hand as she jumps down from the bar. This is why I'm here. The astrophysicist backstory is much more compelling with an actual, practicing physicist in the family.

"My wonderful hubby, the physicist" Bess announces and I grin uncomfortably as I receive a round of undeserved applause. "How do you like the Cab?" she asks in a stage whisper.

"Lavender. Licorice?" I say, holding the glass up to the light and swirling it. "Love it." Den slaps me on the back and everyone laughs.

FOUR

My father looks back at me. Sometimes he's there and sometimes he isn't, but today there's no mistaking the long jawline and wide handles of pre-combed hair trying to escape each temple. He picks the worst days to appear. I walk into the kitchen and Bess looks up from her tablet. I pick up the kettle, weigh it and plug it in.

"That bad?" Bess asks. She knows my hangovers require tea.

"You happy? Was it a success?" She nods without looking up. I lean on the counter and stare at the kettle.

"Den happy with it?" I ask. She looks up. I look back.

"Yes, thank you," she says. "Very happy."

"I'm sure," I say and leave to get dressed. I can pick up tea on my way to work.

I liked Den at first. He was a savvy business partner for Bess. When she, like many new arrivals to southeastern Washington, got into the local wine culture and decided that teaching physics at Washington State University had never been her calling, Den was there for her. Many a Microsoft or Amazon executive decided that their wealth had become sufficiently obscene and that they'd retire to become winemakers, buying 100-acre vineyards with sofa change.

But for us, plowing our meager savings into a vineyard and winery was a very big deal. There's the old adage that to wind up with a small fortune in winemaking you need to begin with a large one. Den gave us a comfort feel that our investment was perhaps unwise, but at least not psychotic. This is the low bar for the wine business so I was grateful to him. I didn't even notice at first that he was targeting more than Bess's enological talents.

The man who had looked back at me from the bathroom mirror was a Den. He might have lacked the business talents, and he knew nothing of wine, but there were some things he and Den had in common. My father had had a long career in promiscuity and it had shaped my life, my mother's and brother's, too. My memories are of anger and misery, and it was cruel of nature to let this DNA hide in my younger self, only to surface and now confront me in the mirror. It may have turned out that physics is quite feckless, but genetics is actually malicious.

I cross town, get onto the Interstate, and take an exit that must mystify most travelers as it seems to lead only to semi-arid wasteland. I merge onto the road that takes you to the site.

I park and check my phone before throwing it onto the passenger seat, leaving it in the car as security protocol requires. Late again. The shift director won't comment. They never do, but I sense that records are being kept. I enter and no one approaches me, not even Kasper. That's a pity since I'd decided to be nice to Kasper today having felt a bit guilty about yesterday. It's unusually quiet. I never did get my tea so I make a beeline for the kitchen.

Something seems wrong. I turn and notice there's no motion in the control room. In fact, no people in the control room. In fact, no people anywhere. I enter the control room. Confirmed. No one. Even the Big Chair is empty. In my years at TMA I'd never seen the Big Chair empty before.

Protocol requires it never be unoccupied except in the instant of a shift change or a toilet break swap-out. I'm panicked and jump into the chair. I have no qualifications or authority to be in this chair but it being empty is worse. I now notice several green lights on the map. Germany, Australia, Venezuela, Japan—two in Japan. Worse still I see a cluster of green. That's an event correlation if I ever saw one. Not good. And what makes it worse than not good is that the cluster is in southeastern Washington state. It's right here. As occupant of the Big Chair I need to order "Affirmative to Echo," but there's no one to say it to. The tachyons are streaming in but I can't do a thing about it. I can't echo them to neutralize the events. I don't know how. It's an art and it's never been my job. I jump up and look into the console from where the echo is triggered, but the controls are soft and not even slightly intuitive. I'm nauseous. What's happening out there? What happened right here? The cold sweat of a hangover has turned to the icy sweat of panic. I'd give up a limb to see a red light right now, but it's all green. Just green. Another green light illuminates.

I need to call someone so I burst out of the control room and run toward my cubicle. Then the Earth shudders and I fall. There's a roar that shakes and deafens me and I clutch onto the ground as the control room glass shatters, cubicle walls collapse and the ceiling lights swing violently. I'm going to be sliced, crushed and buried under a mountain of rubble. I hear myself scream. I hadn't intended to scream but my body knew it was called-for. There was another roar and whatever had been left standing now hit the ground all around me. I cover my eyes as debris rains on me, but it seems light and fragmented rather than heavy and deadly. I look up and the ceiling is still where it should be. If that comes down, it's over. I need to get out of here because where there are two explosions there may be three. I lope toward the main entrance, hurdling over debris. The main door is no longer standing and I run straight out into the parking lot. The other smaller buildings are in various states of collapse. If I'd been in one of those ... The concrete pad of the parking lot is a web of cracks and craters, some a foot across. In all directions I see plumes of rising smoke like a Dickensian landscape of billowing chimneys. Those must be from the elevator shafts and ventilation ducts serving the labyrinth of corridors that navigate the tachyon detector array. I wait but there's no third boom. I notice that my right arm is cut. There's a lot of blood but it doesn't look deep.

Now there's silence but for the geyser of water erupting from one of the collapsed buildings. The detection array has blown up. Why had it taken so long for this to occur to me? An explosion, two explosions, half a mile down is what just happened. But there's nothing in the array that could cause an explosion. So someone did this—blew it up. Something else that had not occurred to me until now is that the parking lot contained a full complement of cars, some of them tilted in craters. I try to focus on the implications, but vomiting comes first.

FIVE

I approach the site gate at the legal speed limit. I need to play this cool—to get out and think. Should I have already called the other Washington? I can't remember the procedure, but I'm pretty sure that I haven't followed it. I need to think. Just think.

I pass the guard house through the exit lane and wave without taking my eyes from the road. They must have felt what just happened and they must see the plumes, but no one tries to stop me. Maybe they're frantically calling the Risley Fire Department. Good luck with that. A fleet of four fire trucks dealing with the aftermath of colossal explosions half a mile deep. That's not one of their drills.

Once there are miles between me and the site fence I take out my cell and call Bess. She may be hearing news of ground-shaking explosions from the site and I need to let her know I'm okay.

"Must be party time!" It's not her. It's a man's voice.

"Who's this?"

"Party Loft. Is it time for a party?" asks the voice without curiosity.

"Sorry," I say and hang up. But that was speed dial. How did I get the ... Party Loft? This time I key in the numbers.

"Must be time for a party—" I hang up and decide to figure this one out later. Now I need to do my job. So what *is* that? I bring up the roster for last night's and this morning's shifts. I start calling, Jenn first. Voice mail. The next name, voice mail. The next name rings out. I look for names that were off-shift. Voice mail. Voice mail. Voice mail. No one there. No one. I tap the cell on my chin. I have to make the call. Protocol requires that only a director can call this number, but protocol probably didn't anticipate this. I take a deep breath and mentally compose a sane opening sentence as I call the number. It rings. It keeps ringing. And keeps ringing. My fear deepens a fathom. This is THE number, our communication trunk with HQ. This number can't just ring out.

So if I'd been on time for my shift ... would my phone be ringing-out too? Where the hell *is* everyone? Who'd be snatching TMA staff and why? And where are they? I'm not going to think the worst.

I need to be somewhere I can think. I can't go home. Why can't I? Because something may be waiting for me there. I used to fear that that something was Den. That was a simpler time. Joe Alvarez has a small place on the river, and now that he's probably wherever the rest of the TMA team are, it'll be available.

I park in his drive and walk around the back of his bungalow. It overlooks the Yakima River, just a few feet from its bank. I shield my eyes to look into the glass porch door. There's no one there and no obvious sign of a struggle. I sit on a porch chair and look at my bloodied arm. There's nothing for it but to break in and find something to clean the wound. It seems security was not at the top of Joe's mind because breaking-in consists of sliding open the porch door and taking a step. The wound is easy to deal with - a couple of band aids. Barely any seepage out of the sides.

I collapse onto the couch and a bag of chips crunches beneath me. I look out the window and the river is serene, oblivious to the circumstances. It flows steadily and calmly while seagulls hover above and a family of ducks paddles by.

So someone has taken out the TMA Tachyon Array team. Why? Do they know what we do? They must; otherwise, why do it? But why do it? What's the motivation? Jenn had always described us as the time police. We enforce the one second per second rule. So with us out of the way, the rule can be broken with impunity. But why would you? I walk to the window and stare out as a dinghy of raucous kids passes by. The why is obvious. I'm so conditioned to think of time acceleration as a disaster to be avoided that I've never given clear thought to what someone might consider an up-side. But the answers are obvious. You could go back a decade with perfect knowledge of the future and make a fortune. I shake my head. But that's wrong thinking, isn't it? One thing TMA has ingrained in me is the complex, inter-related, chaotic, unpredictable consequences of tinkering in the past. Yet someone who hasn't been trained to think that way just wouldn't ... think that way. They'd see the vista of possibilities.

But surely everyone has heard about the paradoxes. Paradox 1: I go back in time and kill my grandfather as a child. So then where did I, the killer, come from? The fact of the matter is that we know all about these paradoxes, but as we look around ourselves, there's no evidence of any weirdness going on. Then again, what would evidence look like? Do we somehow adjust to accommodate it? Maybe these paradoxes are resolving themselves continually right under our noses and we've no way of seeing it. Maybe understanding what's happening means understanding time itself, and we're close to clueless about that. The great Einstein gave us a little false hope for a while, telling us that time is no more than an extra dimension—the fourth one—but all that fell apart, at least for those of us in the know.

So because time's this mystery, what TMA is protecting us from isn't clear. But we know our mission: one second per second, whatever it takes. If we keep that in check, whatever the consequences of forward or backward time acceleration are, we won't need to deal with them. I can live with that. Keep it simple: one second per second. Yet it seems there's someone who can't live with it and the entire team who understands the first thing about any of it has vanished. My first two solid ideas of the morning comes to me. Joe must have tea, and a piece of toast wouldn't go amiss.

My body soaks in the sugar. Whoever these people are, can they reasonably expect to manage time to their benefit? Even I'd be hard-pressed to know how to do that. But that's because I know what I don't know. That's rare knowledge.

Two things happened in the late 1980s. The first was the fuss about *cold fusion*. Until then, fusion was a process deep in a star happening at millions of degrees. It's the ultimate source for all energy and chemical elements. There are attempts to duplicate the conditions in the middle of a star and create a manufactured source of energy for the planet, but we're not there yet. Then along come two chemists (this pains a physicist) who claim they've achieved fusion at room temperature in a big test tube. It's *cold fusion*. That was unbelievable and mostly unbelieved except by credulous journalists.

Around the same time, and much more distressingly, two other scientists find that a reaction involving certain chemicals in certain proportions at certain rates of addition produce a burst of tachyons that accelerates time within a limited burst radius. Whatever object is within that radius is temporally accelerated forward or backward, back then in an uncontrollable way, until it comes to rest at somewhen in the future or the past of when it should have been. They had all the evidence that this was happening, painstakingly analyzed and documented. First it was rudimentary evidence - a glass flask whose design post-dated its first discovery was found sitting on the scientists' lab bench, encrusted in several years-worth of gunk. It was in old photographs. The manufacturers confirmed its production date, although they didn't know why they had been asked. This was crude evidence at first, but then they began to put the pieces together in a rigorous way. The one second per second rule had been violated. Test after test of growing sophistication confirmed what was happening. Quantum coherence analysis, carbon-14 dating, a slew of other methods all cross-validating and confirming each other. And from a chemical reaction of all things: not from some hyper-energetic event like a nuclear blast or a collapsing star, but from boring chemistry in a small, underfunded Midwestern lab.

By this time, like cold fusion, the circles who became privy to the research shrunk drastically. The evidence fed to the broader scientific community justified both findings being laughed off. But in a small inner sanctum, the science of chemo-tachyonics—tackychemistry to most of us—was born. It was the science of time travel, and more importantly, the science of its prevention.

I pace Joe's living room to the extent that the tiny living space allows. What to do now? There are thirty-some people in the world by my count who are close to understanding tackychemistry, and we're the ones with even an outside chance of resolving this catastrofuck. Thirty-some minus one of them are missing. It feels like something can only be up to me. So that's a shame, because I'm clueless. And now that I think about it, being in the home of another TMAer is a really bad idea.

SIX

It's a problem and there's no solution that involves just me. And anyone who could help is now part of the problem. They've gone. So my idea is one of withering stupidity that violates, in word and in spirit, every TMA regulation in the sizable volume that sat on a recently collapsed book shelf. The fact of the matter is that I already have a list of violations to my name; this idea would be just one more. If all came to light, and if the world is not sucked into its own ass of temporal paradoxes, and if I was on trial, I'd just ask for the new crime to be taken into consideration during sentencing. I drive toward home. I know there may be someone waiting for me, but I'm going to take the risk. I have to.

It didn't take long after the discovery of temporal acceleration for the question to be asked—can a person be transported? And it didn't take long after that to try it. There was great care taken that the first hapless volunteer wouldn't be ripped and flung apart—eyes to 1995, spleen to 1912 and gonads to 2500. There was already a growing understanding of how the parameters of the chemical reaction affected the transportation radius, the temporal acceleration rate, and the terminal point. Objects of increasing complexity and structure were used as guineas pigs: a bottle of Perrier, an electric kettle, a microchip, a living plant, a cockroach, then an actual guinea pig if I remember right. And then the first person.

She took no convincing. They aimed for an hour forward, but overshot by a day because it was, and still is, an art. Yet she arrived intact and in rude health. Then, enter the temporal logicians. Different animals altogether from tackychemists. We are entirely focused on the *How?* while the temporal logicians were about the *Why?* and *Why Not?* with emphasis on the latter. After tortuous deliberation, the *Why Not?* could be boiled down to simplicity itself: Because we don't know what the hell could happen. The rest is embellishment. So temporal acceleration became absolutely taboo, and the TMA was born.

The car behind me honks and I look up at the traffic lights. Something, although I can't tell what, is confusing me. I pull into a side street and step out of my car. I look around to get my bearings, reading the street signs and scanning three-sixty for landmarks. I confirm I am where I think I am. So then, why is there a park where there should have been a strip mall?

Thick white cedars, a pathway and park benches border the central rectangle of grass at the center of which is an ornamental basalt column surrounded by flowers. This is where there should have been my favorite Thai restaurant, a barber shop, a bakery, and a movie theater. I drove past them just this morning and I did not drive past a park and a basalt column. My heart races. I look at passers-by. A woman with a dog, teenagers walking hand-in-hand. None of them seem bewildered, looking around themselves in shock. It's only me. Two boys run by me into the park and begin to toss a frisbee. My legs feel shaky and I lean back against my car.

As I drive on I am now looking side-to-side for signs of weirdness, of anomalies. Now and again I convince myself I've seen something—that building was never there before, that crossroad is new—but it's just my paranoid imagination. These things haven't changed.

I get to my neighborhood and slow down to a crawl. Are there cars I don't recognize? Pedestrians in black suits and sunglasses? It all looks normal and I pull into my driveway. Bess's car isn't there. More importantly, neither is Den's. I notice the place is looking a little run down. My fault, of course. I've lived here since childhood and I held onto the place after my parents passed. When I moved back to Risley with my new bride, she was never keen on us living there, but after a while it got comfortable and Bess made the place her own.

I enter and quickly step back out. I look along the street to my left then to my right and then again into the house. It's wrong. But not completely wrong. That's the most disorienting type of wrong. It's dark instead of light, dank instead of fresh. The furniture is in the wrong positions and is the wrong furniture. But I recognize this stuff, or some of it anyway. It's stuff we trashed years ago. Our bright, airy decor is now replaced by my old, dark junk, and a picture window in the back wall has been ... uninstalled. It's oppressive and airless.

I had always assumed that when I was first confronted by a temporal anomaly that I'd think to myself *Of course. That's how these anomalies resolve themselves. It's so obvious. Why didn't I predict that?* But that is not what I'm thinking. I'm bewildered. The other possibility I'd taken on board is that an anomaly would carry me along with it and I'd be oblivious to any weirdness at all. I'd just be part of it. But that isn't happening either because my head and my memories are in how it used to be and not with how it now is.

I remember I'm here on a mission and navigate the

dilapidated furniture toward the main bedroom. At least I assume it's still the main bedroom. It is. It contains an unmade bed and several sticks of furniture that should have been, in fact were, dumped long ago. Instead of the fancy French blue drawer chest that Bess bought there's a bookcase with yellowed, peeling paint. On top of it is not the porcelain Imari vase that had been inherited down generations of Bess's Japanese family, but a flexible desk lamp contorted to illuminate a wall photograph of my mother and brother.

I try to set this all aside. The question is, is it still here? I slide open the closet door and look into the shadows of the interior. All my stuff. Nothing of Bess's. I slide shirts along the wardrobe rail and pull clothing from shelves. Nothing of Bess's. More importantly, I'm not seeing it, the thing I'm here for. I slide the door closed and open the adjacent door. I feel relief as I see it. The safe is half-concealed by draped clothes and I sweep them away. Next question is, is the safe's combination the same? Hand slightly atremble, I jab in the numbers and I'm relieved to hear the whirr of the locks. I exhale, swing open the door and remove the black canvas roll-on bag. I'm about to unzip it when, in the corner of my eye, I detect motion. I turn cold as an exclamation escapes me. There's a figure in the doorway. It takes a step toward me. I squint at it, a silhouette at first.

"Kasper?"

"Hello Joad," Kasper Asmus replies.

"You scared the living crap out of me," I say, fighting a full-body tremble. The room is poorly lit but enough that I begin to notice something. He's not the same. Where yesterday there had been a shock of pale brown hair, there is now a receding hairline and a deeply creased forehead. Heavy bags hang from his eyes and the jawline that had been crisp a day before now sags. Yesterday Kasper was a decade younger than me, and now it looks like the age gap has reversed. He stares.

"What's happening?" I ask. "Do you know?" He blinks

but doesn't answer. "Where's the team?" I take a step toward him and he takes a step backwards.

"All seems a long time ago," he says quietly, to himself more than to me. He looks around the half-lit room and I sense he's as discomposed as me. "Should have known Joad Bevan keeps his own schedule." He shakes his head slowly.

"What's a long time—?" He removes a pistol from his pocket. I gasp and back up against the closet door. He doesn't point it at me, just holds it by his side. I want to look into his face but my eyes are frozen on the weapon. He follows my stare and looks down at the pistol. Then he apologizes. It may be an apology for terrifying me, or an apology for what he's about to do. My heart thuds hard against my ribs and my eyes dart around the room looking for a way out.

"Let's talk about this Kasper. Don't know what the hell's happening but I think we're the only ones left to fix it," I say between sharp breaths. "Let's you and me just figure this out." He raises the gun, points it at my chest, and reaches with his other hand for the slide lock. Then his brow furrows. The slide is stuck? Without thought and the time that that would waste, I launch myself at him and he topples backwards, the battered bookshelf collapsing under our weight. I grope for the fallen lamp and grab it by its arm, then swing its base into his face. He's pushing back on my chest, looking around himself for the pistol. I bring down the lamp base on his face again. And again. He has stopped struggling, a steady stream of red gushing from the bridge of his nose. And again. I'm panting but I seem to be as steady as a rock. No shakes. No panic. When you're about to be finished-off, it seems a sharp sense of pragmatism descends on you. Have I killed him? No, he's breathing, but he's out cold. I get to my feet and see that the gun is right by his chest, too close for him to have seen. I take deep breaths, exhaling slowly through pursed lips. That needs to go with me. I pick up the gun.

I back away from Asmus's body, extend the handle of

the roll-on bag, unzip a compartment and slip the pistol into it. The bloodied Kasper Asmus is motionless. "Block mathematical notation," I whisper. "Asshole."

SEVEN

I'm sitting just by the bar, or where I think the Thai restaurant bar would have been if it hadn't been replaced by a park. The warm Risley sun gifts me a moment of serenity, painting a vanilla glow on my closed eyelids. The roll-on case is by my knees and I sit on the park bench feeling like I'm waiting for my flight to be called. And this will be an epic flight.

I try to reconstruct the last hour. A middle-aged Kasper Asmus tries to kill me in my house—a version of my house, anyway. If there was ever any doubt we're dealing with temporal acceleration then the middle-aged Kasper Asmus removed it. Right? Of course. But where does a middle-aged Kasper Asmus come from? He could have accelerated back from a time twenty or thirty years out where he *is* middle-aged. Or maybe he accelerated backwards from here and just aged his way back to 2021. Or maybe one of another hundred variations. And this all begs the question of why he wanted to shoot me. Sure, we never got on, but ...

A white ball with red spots rolls up to my feet and a small girl looks up for permission to take it back. Her mother smiles at me apologetically having mistaken rumination for irritation. I smile and hand the ball back. Now, my house.

I'd say that what that house was, was a house with no sign of Bess. None of her clothes or other stuff was there, and the decor was what had made her weep when she first saw it. It looked to me like the house it would have been if untouched by Bess. Okay, so that's the beginnings of an explanation. But why? How? I'm rapidly discovering that thinking is not the help I thought it'd be.

I get to my feet. My plan is a dizzying violation of all that TMA stands for. My plan is to change history. It's to commit the evil of going back, but to do it to undo a bigger evil. That's my rationale. It's a rationale that temporal logicians—TLs—have long rejected. They say, *benevolent tinkering can only make things worse in unpredictable ways. Good intentions are no defense. Don't do it. And furthermore, DON'T DO IT.* One second per second is the only tick rate that's acceptable. Period. But in reality, TLs are philosophers of the most clueless kind. Anyone who's seen *Back To The Future* more than once has as much understanding of temporal logic as any TL. I'm going back, and if in future, or past, I need to face the music, then so be it.

The privacy I need is a short walk down to the Columbia riverbank. I arrive at a clearing in the middle of a thicket of wild olive trees, unzip the main compartment of my roll-on bag and take out the ribbed metal case about a foot squared and half as high. I lay it on the ground, flip open the latches and remove its content: a temporal accelerator. It looks like a chunky, old hand-held programmable controller resting on an oval container attached along one side to three metal bulbs. It looks like this because that's exactly what it is. Not going for the elegance a Steve Jobs might have insisted upon, TMA made a few of these years ago with the idea that human temporal acceleration might be a last resort fix for some big problem caused by dumbass nature. The least of all evils argument still held sway back then, before the TLs weighed-in. When TMA saw the error of its ways it ordered the accelerators destroyed. Problem was, they hadn't thought ahead to carefully count how many of them had been assembled, and this one, via a lineage of TMA staff, had made its way to me and to my bedroom safe.

Each bulb contains one of the three offending chemicals that, when combined in the correct proportions, and in the right order and at the specified addition rates, conspire to mock the very laws of physics. 6-phenyl-5H-pyrrolo[4,5-a]pyrazine-5,7(6H)-dione is one of them. I committed this to memory just to see if I could, and also to remind myself of the banal complexity of chemistry. The names of the other two chemicals were too long for me to even attempt memorization, but I know colleagues who had them down cold. Colleagues now missing. But no complaint from me about the complexity and rarity of these chemicals because that's why we have just a few green dots a day lighting up on the wall map, and not hundreds or even thousands. Nature may be an imbecile, but not imbecilic enough to decide a mixture of vinegar and baking powder should explode like a tachyon firework. Yet all the events that lit up the green dots, at least in my experience at TMA, were innocent ones where these rare chemicals were brought together by some hapless researcher in the exact Goldilocks proportions.

The oval container on the accelerator is the reaction chamber connected to the three chemical bulbs by micro-injectors, programmed from the controller. Programming the accelerator is, in principle, straightforward. The two parameters to set are the tachyon inner blast radius and the termination point. The inner blast radius is what sizes the sphere of matter that gets caught up in the acceleration. The termination point is where you wind up timewise. This does sound elegantly simple, the flaw being that, as far as I know, this thing has the accuracy of the first musket. There never came a chance to refine it before it became taboo.

A week should do it, I think. Show up, work with Jenn and the other directors, get HQ involved. Track down the explosives that had been planted in the sensor array. Maybe even catch the bastards planting them. Be waiting for whoever shows up to take out the TMA team. Does that plan make sense? A week? Maybe a month is safer? Like this thing has that kind of accuracy. I'll set it for a week back and let *it* decide. I then point my trembling finger at the 'Activate' key. Am I going to feel like I'm being dragged through a wormhole, ripped apart by gravitational tides? Or like I'm being disassembled quark by quark, electron by electron, and crushed back together in a vice? I hear my heart thudding fast as I touch 'Activate'.

EIGHT

What I actually sense is a slight fall in the ambient light level. There are clouds where there had been none. Was that it? Shouldn't I be at least slightly disoriented? I've been known to vomit just looking at a painting of a boat yet time acceleration does nothing to me? I check my cell to see if I've landed anywhere close to my target, but it's still showing the same time and date. Yet something has definitely changed, if only the weather. I pack up the accelerator and tow my roll-on bag up the slope from the river. Nothing looks too strange so I know I haven't shot myself back a millennium. The cars look flatter, less cockroachlike. They have the style of junkers, yet shiny and new. I reach the place where there should be a park. Or a strip mall. There is neither, just an expanse of Russian thistle weed trapped by wire fencing. I have the tingling in the pit of my stomach that I haven't felt since I was a kid. It's the feeling of being lost. I check my cell again for a signal. Could I be predating a cell tower? I kick my bag. "Piece of shit." I've overshot the one week I was going for, and by a lot is what I'm guessing. What are my options? I could try to get back to the place I started out, but god knows where I'd actually wind up.

A thought occurs to me. TMA. Is there a TMA yet? If there is, I'd at least have someone I could talk to. But if this is earlier than 1991, I'm out of luck. TMA was the Manhattan Project of its era. As soon as the catastrophe potential of chemo-tachyonic reactions was realized, it was time for serious steps to be taken and the federal government took them. The curtain of secrecy came down and the handful of physicists who had some clue about the science of it were vetted and cordoned off. Then they kept it small. Always small. The fewer people who had a clue about what was happening, the better. A dozen people in DC and thirty-some in Washington state was how it was and how it stayed. That's how many people knew what was going on. The question is, are some of those people right up the street from here, yet?

I see a public phone. It takes coins. Who carries coins? I see the Brookland Avenue sign. I know there are a few stores up there, maybe. Yes, the first is a dry cleaner. It looks familiar.

"Hello, can I help you?" a smiling pixie-faced woman with cropped yellow hair asks while looking at my case, eager for me to remove the laundry it should contain. The shop is brightly lit and a conveyor of plastic-bagged clothing is moving behind her.

"Hi. Uh, yes," I stutter. "Could I ask you a big favor?" Her smile fades as if she now recognizes me as what I am. Just one in a stream of bums here to ask a favor, like using her toilet or her telephone. "I don't have any change for the phone and really need to make a call." She stares at me, unsympathetically. "Just a local one. Really quick."

"We're not allowed to let the public use the phone."

"I know, of course not," I turn my smile up a little but not enough to seem smarmy. "If it wasn't an emergency ... It'd be such a help." She surveys me for a moment then nods to the wall phone. I put together my palms to acknowledge my answered prayer, and as I pick up the handset I see the wall calendar by its side. March, 1996. I look down at my roll-on case. "Piece of shit," I hiss then mouth *not you* at the pixie woman.

Now, this better be the same number. I shield my mouth with a cupped hand and look back at the pixie who still has me in her glare. Add calling TMA on a nonsecured line to my list of charges. A woman answers. "Hello."

"I need to speak to the onshift director," I say.

After a pause, "I'm sorry, what did you say?"

"I'm TMA and I need to speak to the onshift director." Again, a pause, this time longer.

"Hello," a different female voice says.

"Are you the onshift director?"

"Who is this?"

"My name's Joad Bevan. I'm with TMA." I turn to the pixie. "This is very private, sorry. I'll be off in a minute. Really." The pixie gives me a theatrically cynical look then walks back among the hanging clothes bags.

"I don't know a Joad Bevan," the voice replies. I might as well go for broke.

"No, you wouldn't. I've accelerated back from 2021 and I have a problem." Then the longest pause yet. If that didn't get her attention, what would?

"Where are you?" she asks. I read her the address stamped on the generic drycleaner's calendar. "Are you safe?"

Although I knew I was lost, it hadn't occurred to me until now that I might not be safe. "I think I am."

"Stay there." She hangs up.

NINE

Almost an hour passes before a red Chevy van pulls up outside. I step out and the passenger window opens to reveal a shiny, pink-faced man with military cut ginger hair who looks me up and down. The back door slides opens and he beckons me. The driver, a wiry older woman in a leather security windbreaker walks arounds the van and puts my case in the back.

Without a word exchanged, we pull out. After a few minutes the pink-faced man turns back to me and asks for ID. I hand over my TMA ID.

"What's this?" he asks.

"TMA credential," I reply. His stare is a potpourri of suspicion, contempt and militaristic efficiency.

"No it isn't," he says.

"Not yet." He keeps the credential and turns away. The ride out of Risley is familiar yet alien. Someone once said that the past is a foreign country. They were never in my particular situation but they had it right. I lived here–live here–in 1996. With force, it suddenly hits me that I'm a few miles from here–a ten year-old me, that is. How can that be? You can be in the time acceleration business a long time, but you don't experience the full bewilderment of it until the ten year-old you is a few miles away.

Once out into the semi-arid wastelands, the landscape becomes more familiar, less changed. The driver speaks inaudibly to the site gate guard and we travel on. So here is TMA circa 1996. Same building but maybe a little newer and shinier. Other than the old model cars in the parking lot, it could be where I arrived this morning. I shiver.

The cigarette fumes are what I notice first, then the conversations. There's chatter within cubicles, chatter across cubicles, and a gathered group laughing. They all seem quite talkative, even friendly, very *un*-TMA. And it looks like plaid shirt and jeans is the uniform. I'm led to the meeting room, which now contains a battered metal-framed, Formica-surfaced table surrounded by a dozen school chairs. The pink-faced man who I now see is no older than his late twenties points me to a chair. The driver brings in the case and shuts the door to our windowless conference room. She unzips it and puts its contents on the far end of the table. An accelerator and an automatic pistol. Pink-face stares at the pistol and then at me. It seems I'm expected to answer a question he hasn't asked. I wonder if that type of gun doesn't yet exist. I know zip about guns. Or maybe it's just a matter of, *why the hell do you have a gun?* The door opens, a woman and a man enter. The woman dismisses my escorts with a *thank you.* They whisper something to her, hand her my credential, then take the accelerator and the gun with them. She smiles once they leave. Her smile is a small thing but it warms me. Someone who doesn't have contempt for me—yet.

"We spoke on the phone," she says in a voice that's husky yet precise, with a touch of the South. She pours a glass of water from a jug and places it in front of me. She's lean and outdoorsy looking—a cyclist or climber maybe. About my age, a face that relaxes to a smile, freckles, intelligent blue eyes and light brown hair tied back into a tight bun.

"So tell me," she says, sitting down across from me.

"Starting where, when?" I ask. She shrugs. "It's your story." The man who had entered with her had no intention of going along with the patient approach.

"What's your name again?" he asks sharply. He also looks about my age, heavily bespectacled, with unkempt, black greasy hair. He has a sardonic expression that promises whatever I reply will be a setup for him.

"Joad Bevan," I say.

"And where are you from?" he asks.

"Here." I reply to the woman. "Born and raised in Risley." They exchange a glance.

"Yes, we looked you up," he says. "You're ten years old." She places her hand on his arm in the way that says *shut up.*

"You can imagine we're a little confused," she says.

"I need your help," I say. I'm not used to being so direct when I'm not talking about matters of science, but I had breathed in and that's what had come out. The woman leans forward, puts her palms down on the table and smiles at me. I exhale slowly.

"So start at the beginning Joad Bevan," she says. My mind dissolves into the fog of the day's events: the big hangover, the big boom, the world shift, the gun in my chest, and the incompetent workings of a junk accelerator. I sip my water and feel a tremble in my hand, so put the glass down quickly, hoping it wasn't noticed. I compose myself and belatedly return the woman's smile. Then I tell them the epic tale of my day. Not the hangover, not the confrontation with Bess—not relevant—but from there on I share every detail I can remember. I'd told my story to the tabletop but now look up into the face of the woman. With her faint, natural smile she is looking back at me. Her greasy partner has a look that's on the verge of a sneer or a roll of the eyes, but he does neither. I sit back in my seat to say, *well that's it.* The man and woman exchange a glance.

"I'm Jane Galois, the shift director. This is Boris Zhivov." I look up with a start.

"Zhivov?" I say. He nods. This little shit is the Director of TMA, or at least he will be. I'd met him once years ago (years from now) when he visited the site. This is the same guy? I suppose that before thirty added pounds, an expanding forehead, and a jawline victim to gravity, this could be him. Director Zhivov did make some decisions only a schmuck could make, so now that all makes sense. It occurs to me that I'm judging the young Zhivov on nothing he's said, and just on how he looks. Well, that's Joad Bevan for you. Am I supposed to say nothing to him about who he is? There are no rules about that because bigger rules should prevent the question from even arising.

"You're convincing, Joad Bevan," the woman says. "Anything to add?"

"How about a song?" I say and slide my iPhone across the table.

TEN

They allow me to look around. Some things are as they were (as they will be) and some are not. I peer through the control room window and where there had been a wall-sized monitor, there are now four large TV screens positioned to share the world map. There's a single red light illuminated somewhere in central Europe. What luxury. That'd be a hell of a good day where I'm from. One light! The big chair is occupied by a lean, gray-haired man in a golf tee-shirt and he's transfixed on the four monitors, despite the little action they're showing. The consoles now have hard controls rather than touch screens but are laid-out about the same. I think these old consoles were still there when I started work.

It gets me thinking to when I first entered this place, fifteen years from now. Bess had been confused by why, after working for years toward an escape from Risley, that I was so eager to return. There was a cover story for all TMAers about the site being there as an academic enterprise for the detection of exotic fundamental particles. I convinced Bess that this excited me so she found a research job at Washington State University and Risley became our home. It all seems an age away, in one direction or the another.

I remember my first day. My heart had pounded with the excitement of being there, of being one of the elite. But the exhilaration I had felt was also part relief, having successfully gone through the grueling process of vetting. It's not that I was worried about anything they might turn up in my background, but I'd been warned that some pretty strange things could disqualify me: things like being a sci fi reader or having been involved in role-play games. Go figure. But I guess I'd ticked all the boxes despite the occasional Asimov. Most of the vetting had taken place before I even knew I was in the running. I'm still not sure how I got singled-out. A PhD in theoretical physics at 21 and a few well received papers in the field of particle phenomenology must have had something to do with it. I'd asked my boss, once I felt comfortable with it, *what if I hadn't wanted the job after all that vetting?* He'd replied *you mean what if you'd wanted a job with more interesting science or more relevant to the benefit of mankind?*

I recall the smell on that first day, which in hindsight I think was just the plastic furniture. But on that day, my identity changed. I was no longer Joad Bevan, physicist, but now Joad Bevan of TMA, and that went everywhere with me. Standing in a grocery store, at a road crossing or in an airport line, I thought to myself, even though no one knows it, here stands Joad Bevan, TMA.

On day one I had received a dump of technical reports and papers, was pointed to a cubicle, and given the instruction *learn that*. It scared the feces out of me. To come up to speed in a field about which you have zero knowledge is scary, but when that field borders on the incredible, it's terrifying. In my time I had read a lot of papers sent by what we used to call *cranks*. These are amateurs who send their profound ideas on fundamental physics to established theoreticians, despite the fact that their knowledge of physics comes mainly from Star Trek or from a popular book or two on gee-whiz science. Now, reading these papers, they were so *out-there* that it was sometimes tough not to lapse into the mindset that I was reading crank literature. But whoever wrote these papers, they were no cranks. I was assigned a couple of staff to answer questions, and I had a lot.

After a few weeks I was set my first task and my terror level ratcheted. I was told to renormalize a quantized tachyonic field theory on a curved spacetime manifold. It was a stupefyingly scary project and I knew that my assured abject failure would get me thrown out on my ass. I knew it'd expose me as a fake who was way out of his league. Yet, I got it done, and in less than a month. I could exhale.

ELEVEN

There's some fascination with me around the cubicles and there are guarded attempts to draw me into the ambient, amicable banter. Of all the differences between the now now and the future now, it's the easy and cordial chitter-chatter. What sullen, arrogant, and suspicious shits we had become. But why? I find myself irritated by the banter, the good-humored ribbing, and the general friendliness of it all. A few of them try to wheedle from me facts about the future, about *their* future. Galois and Zhivov deflect most of them with mild admonitions. I assure one happy and garrulous woman that all charges against her were ultimately dropped. Her face falls and I give her a *nah, kidding* look.

The rest of the afternoon is technical talk. Not necessarily about the problem at hand, but general chemo-tachyonics. There are things I know that they don't, but not that many. After all, by 2021 we were standing on the shoulders of giants, but with the rising influence of the temporal logicians and the restrictions they were handing down, future TMAers wouldn't be so much standing on the shoulders of giants as being trapped under the feet of hobbits.

Of all the shift staff I recognize no more than two as

younger versions of the team I know, three if you count Zhivov. Physics, especially on the theoretical side, is a young person's sport and TMA staff turnover is high, yet I still would have expected to see more familiar but rejuvenated faces. Retirement from TMA is a tricky matter. We enter the job with exhilaration and pride and then exit our short careers having been battered down by the monstrous responsibility of keeping the one second per second rule while not really understanding the apocalyptic price of failure. Then getting out is as grueling as getting in, when it's made clear that if a word of your old job is leaked, then woe betide you and all things dear to you. When you retire, you sign a piece of paper and then TMA wields its shady power to get you placed in a new job suitable for the husk of a TMAer. And this is the career that chose me, except that my career has placed me in a temporal quagmire and I've responded to it by breaking most of the rules I can remember.

I look around until exhaustion hits me. Onsite accommodations are perfunctory: army cot, stocked fridge, filled food cupboard, microwave oven, a Formica-surfaced table and a school chair. These rooms are still used in my time, set up for anyone who needs to pull an all-nighter and in need of a power nap. My head touches the pillow and it's morning.

TWELVE

"And it came to pass that the awaited one appeared." The voice is male, but it's soft and in a high register. This is a more Messianic start to a day than I'd expected. Galois had escorted me back into the meeting room which now contains Zhivov and a man I haven't met. I sit.

"This is Ram Prasad," Galois says. I do a double take but try to disguise it with a stretch of my neck. *Give me a break* is what I'm thinking. Today's shocks to the system have already begun. Ram Prasad is/was the stuff of legend—Einstein-league—except that only the *inner sanctum* would have heard of him. But within TMA, Ramesh Prasad was Einstein and Edison rolled into one: unparalleled theoretician, but also brilliant practician and inventor. Not many physicists have ticked either of those boxes, and a vanishingly small number have ticked both: Isaac Newton, Enrico Fermi, then Ram Prasad is the list I'd make. I look at Galois who is smiling back.

"An honor to meet you," I say feebly. "I'm Joad Bevan." I hold out my hand and Prasad looks at me, as if wondering why I'd think the occasion called for that, but he obliges me with a brief, limp grasp.

"I know who you are," he says. "So tell me what you've

learned." What have I learned? When? From whom? I look to Galois and Zhivov but they offer no help.

"Are you asking me how I got here?" I say. There's impatience in Prasad's face.

"I know how you got here." He points to the sheets of paper in front of him. "I'm asking what you've learned. You've just gone through something you've never been through before. What did you learn from it?" This is the sort of question that usually gets a smartass answer from me, but Prasad's ass is much smarter than mine and I make an exception.

"I don't know what you're asking me," I say. Prasad sighs. Galois and Zhivov remain no help and seem embarrassed on my behalf. Prasad consults the notes in front of him. He gives me a look that says, *okay, then I'll spoon feed you my questions if that's what I have to do.*

"You noted that in 2021 you found yourself in a park where you expected there to be a shopping mall: where there had been a shopping mall that very morning." Prasad is reading through the glasses perched on the end of his nose and then looks up above them, directly at me. I nod. "Must have come as a surprise."

"To put it mildly," I say. *You have a powerful grasp on the obvious* is what my reply to anyone else would have been.

"Any observations about that?" Prasad looks as if he's rooting for me to give the right answer and to stop embarrassing myself, as if he's doing his very best for me. How lucky I am, I think. I never got a chance to make a fool of myself in front of Ram Prasad when he was alive, but now fate is giving me a second chance.

"Are you asking about the temporal logic of it?"

"If you want to look at it that way," he replies dismissively. "I'm just asking you to think rationally and tell me what you have concluded given your recent experiences, Dr. Bevan." This is a level of mortification I'm unused to. "There were people in the park," he says, consulting the notes. I nod. "And did they seem shocked, astounded, seized by wonderment?" My neck warms by twenty degrees.

"No, they didn't," I reply. "But *I* was shocked and astounded."

"Ah," says Prasad to his imbecilic student who at last seems to have inched forward his side of the conversation.

"And why would that be?" I ask on his behalf. "Why would they just take the existence of the park in their stride, while to me, it's a park that came out of nowhere?" Prasad's expression is one of *thank god for that*. "What's different about them? About me?" I feel a cynical grin from Zhivov yet when I turn to him, there's only rapt attention.

"And the answer?" Prasad asks. I shake my head. I don't know the answer. "I was at the tachyon detection array when it was blown up. Is that what—"

"Why would that make a difference?" Prasad asks. I have no answer. "I don't know why that would make a difference."

"Think about your timeline—" Galois says.

"No Gallie," Prasad interrupts. "Let Dr. Bevan from the future figure this out. Someone thought he was TMA material. Unless recruitment standards plummet by 2021, he can think this through for himself." At this Prasad shifts his notes aside. "But no rush. Let's move on." I lean forward into whatever discussion is coming next, but it seems Prasad's announcement was a sign to get rid of me while serious conversation could begin. Zhivov escorts me from the meeting room and closes the door behind me. And there I stand: a man who has disgraced himself in front of the greatest scientific mind of the late twentieth century.

THIRTEEN

I relive that meeting a dozen times. I entered as the Messiah
(for reasons I've not been told) and exit the simpleton. My
mother had a way with words, and there was a word that, as
far as I know, only she used for the type of off-the-scale
embarrassment I had just experienced. It was *shitten*. I feel
truly shitten. For several days there's no relief. I'm so used
to treating temporal logic with scorn, as does my whole tribe
of tackychemists, I hadn't been thinking clearly about the
questions Prasad had posed. What should have occurred to
my befuddled mind is that everything has changed. His
question wasn't about theoretical temporal logic, the sort
that TLs spend a career jerking off to. He wanted an opinion
on what was now actual experimental temporal logic. I had
lived it, yet all I could do was drool, slack-jawed, and admire
the mystery. But the fact of the matter is that I still can't
answer his question. Why would I be the only one who
knows that that Risley park wasn't meant to be there while
the kids playing in it and the families walking through it gave
no hint of bewilderment. What's special about me? And
then, what's it like for one of those oblivious people in the
park? Does having a history that's suddenly altered cause no
sensation? I can't think this through. Maybe it takes a Ram

Prasad. Not being the smartest one in the room is a new sensation for me, and I don't like it.

For the following days the meeting room door stays shut. Prasad, Galois and Zhivov are sequestered in there with the occasional TMA staffer visiting. I spend my time milling around the cubicle area or pressing my nose to the control room window. I'm of no use to anyone. You'd think a guy from the future would have some value, but beyond trying to wheedle out of me information about their future lives, there was no interest in me. I even considered garnering a little attention by stirring up interest in the plot lines of future *Friends*.

I watch the shift directors rotate through the big chair. There's the lean, ex-military-looking grayhair. He's a hypercritical, sarcastic bastard who takes pleasure in making his team feel stupid. He'd fit right in in 2021 TMA, but here, he's the exception to the rule. Another shift director is an amiable older guy whose belt is lost beneath an overhanging belly and whose thin wisps of sandy hair bounce with every stride. Galois is the third shift director but she's hidden away with Prasad and Zhivov, so her deputy sits in the chair. The deputy is a waif of a woman lost in her baggy shirts and jeans who wears thick-rimmed, black eyeglasses that conceal her features but for a long, slender nose and a thin-lipped, unsmiling mouth. She seems sharp as a tack, and not a spare word exits her.

By the standards of the TMA I know, there's little action in the control room. Maybe one green light per day. Some days none at all. I start to spend more time in my quarters, just sitting on my bed and listening to the radio. In an act of compassion, someone had brought a TV into my room. It's unsettling to think that another copy of me may be watching exactly the same TV shows a few miles away. I am truly useless, it seems, unworthy even of being told why I'm being kept waiting, and for what.

FOURTEEN

Galois stands outside the open door to my room. This hasn't happened before. Her hair is let down, framing her face and resting on her shoulders. I realized I had looked at her for too long. She sees the TV before I can fire my remote.

"Is it the one where Rachel shows up wearing her wedding dress?" she asks with plausible interest. It is, but better not to acknowledge it.

"It's nice to receive a visit, I say. "By anyone," I add.

"Want to go for a ride?"

"I want to do anything that's gets me out of this tin hut," I reply. I follow her and we're soon seated in her maroon, beat-up Volvo wagon.

"Thanks for being patient," she says after a couple of miles.

"You're thanking me for being something I'm not," I reply. We cross miles of desert and eventually enter the outskirts of town.

"How familiar is it all?" she asks. "Is it as you remembered it?" We're southbound toward the center of Risley, to the extent that one big suburb has a center.

"Sort of. There are things I'd forgotten I'd

remembered." I see the ice cream parlor where my friends and I used to congregate after school to exchange outrageous and false stories of sexual adventure.

"I guessed there'd be things you wanted to see," she says. We exchange a glance and she smiles. I notice for the first time the soft, musical timbre of her voice. Maybe it's a voice she doesn't use when Prasad and Zhivov are in earshot.

"There are. But more than that, I want to know what happens next," I say. I've surprised myself by getting back to business because I was enjoying that moment in which the steel cords under my skin were beginning to melt. "Are you going to help me make all of this right?" She raises her eyebrows at this but doesn't reply, and no more is said until we turn the corner onto Walla Walla Street.

I see that the shingles on my single story house has a fresh coat of yellow paint. There are two boys in the front yard behind the chain-link fence playing catch. They're wearing swimsuits and catchers mitts, and they're laughing hysterically as they try to outrun the rotating sprinkler while making their catch. I take a deep breath. One of them is me. My little brother Tom is the other. Galois pulls in to park on the opposite side of the street. We're both so lean; no, we're plain skinny. Tom screams as my pitch forces him into the sprinkler spray. I laugh with joy and exhilaration.

"Thank you, Jane" I whisper.

"Everyone calls me Gallie." *Gallie*, I echo distractedly, without turning. "This must feel very weird."

"It feels like *Christmas Carol* when Scrooge visits himself as the young man without a care."

"Does that make me the Ghost of Christmas Past?" I'm about to reply when a woman steps out from the house, sits on the front steps and joins in the laughter. Her hazelnut hair is pulled into a ponytail and she's wearing a pale green tank top, khaki shorts and is barefoot. She puts on a blue baseball cap and pulls her ponytail through the back. How did I forget that? That was her favorite Mariners cap. She's so young. Why do I never remember her this way? "She's beautiful," Gallie says and I nod.

"Think it's okay if I get out?" I ask.

"Better not."

I want to run over to her. Hug her. But she probably wouldn't take that well. We watch them play for a while, then without warning Joad looks my way and our eyes lock. What can he be seeing? Then the sprinkler spray hits him and there are peals of laughter. I laugh too. But when I exhale, the air takes the joy with it. "She'll be dead within five years," I say, not really to Gallie.

"I'm sorry," she whispers.

"Not a happy life. You'd never know it looking at her now, would you?" We sit and watch for a few minutes longer before I ask Gallie to drive on. I thank her and we sit in silence as I stare out of the side window to conceal myself.

"Joad," Gallie says eventually, "there's a lot you don't know."

"Then tell me."

"Your TMA team are alive," she says. "And we need to get them back." I turn to her.

"Back from where?" She hesitates.

"Centuries away, but we can get them." *Centuries away?*

"What—"

"You're right to be cynical about temporal logic, Joad. It *is* a dark art, but we know a lot more than we used to. We know that when things get messed up, there are some strategies to fix them that aren't going to work without making everything worse, and there are others ways with a better chance." I now remember the cluster of green lights centered on southeastern Washington just before the wall map shattered into a thousand shards and rained down. Those green lights were the TMA team being flung—*centuries away*.

"Tell me what's going on Gallie," I plead.

"Soon," she says. "I can't yet. I'm sorry. I just can't." I look back out of the side window. "But hey," she says, "I've got a suggestion. You must be going slightly crazy in your jail cell. How would you like to move out?"

"Where to? And yes, whatever your answer is."

"Well, Boris has offered you his spare bedroom."

"Zhivov?"

"Yes, he has a nice little house down on the Yakima River with plenty of room. What do you think?" I think back to Joe Alvarez's house down on the Yakima where I hid out after the site explosion. "Hey, don't embarrass yourself. Rein in your excitement."

"I didn't think he liked me."

FIFTEEN

Zhivov's home becomes my home. It's in surprisingly good taste for a man I'd assumed lived under his parents' stairs. At first the routine didn't call for us being in much contact. Day at TMA, pick up a carry-out on the way home, eat mainly in silence then retire to our respective rooms. I tried to probe for information a couple of times but he's airtight. I guess you don't get to become the TMA Director without being a good corporate man. And the new fact that has entered my fog of bewilderment seems to subtract from, rather than add to, my grasp on the situation—that my TMA team are centuries away. *Centuries away!*

It's a Friday night and it's after a couple of store-bought beers that Zhivov crushes his empty can and suddenly looks like a man who has something to tell me.

"Would you say TMA does a good job?" he asks. Okay, a weird question that did not follow-on from the topic of noisy geese. "How many green lights would you say we get a day?"

"Up to twenty. At least where I'm from. Here, a couple a day maybe, at most."

"And do you think we're detecting *all* acceleration events?"

I nod. "That's the idea, isn't it?" Zhivov pops another beer.

"Say you wanted to mask an event, conceal it from detection, how would you do it?"

"I guess I'd try to confine the tachyon blast—attenuate the tachyon emission beyond the inner blast radius." Zhivov nods.

"How?"

"Reflectors. Absorbers. But who the hell would know how to configure that? You'd need to be TMA. A tackychemist, and a pretty good one. Hands-on type."

"Maybe," says Zhivov. "So, do you think that TMA is airtight enough that that would never happen? That it hasn't happened? Maybe deliberately. Maybe through technology leakage? And that the green lights on the map don't account for *every* acceleration?"

"You're saying it could be going on and we can't see it?"

"I'm saying it *is* going on." I cut short a gulp and stare at Zhivov.

"Who? Why?"

"Why? Isn't it obvious, Toad?" This had become Zhivov's name for me during our growing detente. I still called him Boris, not having been able to think of anything funnier. If there's any silver lining to my situation it's being able to insult the man who will one day hold such power over me.

"Who's insane enough to think they could profit from screwing around with acceleration when outcomes are completely uncontrollable?"

"Well, that brings us to the other factor." Zhivov says. "Sheer craziness. Someone who wants to violently shake up everything just for the sake of doing it. Time vandals." *Time vandals!* "Assholes," Zhivov clarifies.

"Kasper Asmus is an asshole," I say. "His headshot is in the dictionary under 'asshole'. Is he a time vandal? Is that what's going on?" I shake my head. "No, that's too insane. Someone who's a time vandal is running the risk of destroying themselves, no?"

"That's why 'asshole' doesn't come close. They generally just don't care. The power is the thing. Don't get me wrong, Toad, TMA does a good job. But TMA is all about prevention—stopping acceleration before it can get started—and you know what they say about an ounce of prevention. The reality is, we still need to have a cure."

"Cure?"

"Yes. Human acceleration *does* happen without TMA detecting it. That's just a fact. Then the cure is whatever it takes to undo whatever our vandal does. Mend the damage."

"How?"

"You know how. We need to accelerate, too," Zhivov says in a whisper.

"But—"

"But that would break our own rules?" Zhivov says. I nod. "The rules handed down to us by the temporal logicians? By the way, I think you're too hard on those guys, Toad. They were just following orders."

"Meaning?"

"Meaning once we knew that masked accelerations were happening, we needed to shut down acceleration technology. Ban the whole fucking thing. And the logicians came in handy. Dumb as rocks, I know, but they were useful. The reality is, we had to improve acceleration technology to administer the cure."

"TMA did?"

"Well, yes and no," Zhivov says. "Not TMA. At least not all of it. Not officially."

I shake my head. "Not all of it? Then ... who?"

"A few of us."

"A few of you." I digest this. The few among the few. And whatever happened in 2021 is something we need to cure?"

"Damn right we do."

"You know I had a plan," I say. "I traveled back to give

my own cure a shot: warning the site staff and preventing it all from happening in the first place. But my piece of shit accelerator—"

"We know that, Toad. You were trying to cut it off at the pass so it never even happened. But we've discovered a few things. Some things just won't work."

"And mine won't?"

"Yours didn't. What we know is that you need to follow the timeline, not prevent it. That's where the cure lies."

"Follow it?"

"Yes, recover from what's been done."

"And how do we *recover* from what's been done?"

"We find your team and we rescue them."

"Rescue them? Rescue them from what?"

Zhivov pulls something from his pocket and hands it to me. It's a round, silver-framed photograph about the size of a drinks coaster. I look closer, and under cracked glass it's a black silhouette on white of a woman with long eyelashes, receding chin and stacked hair. *Marge Simpson* is what I think. "Found it. Beautiful isn't it?" he says. "Shame it's damaged. When would you date that to?"

"I don't know. The days of yore," I reply. "What is it?" Zhivov shrugs and then shuts down as suddenly as he had opened up. It's then I realize that every word he'd uttered had more to do with Prasad than with the beer.

SIXTEEN

Tonight I have the dream again. It's one of those dreams that you know is a dream. And in it, every time, I remember that I've been having this dream all my life. How could I have forgotten it? Its familiarity is overwhelming, as if it's more my world than anything I've experienced awake–as if leaving the dream is always just an excursion, a temporary escape from this reality. Or perhaps believing that the dream recurs is just part of the dream–this single dream for a single night that pretends it has known me for a lifetime. And when I wake up I know it will be gone. It always is.

The dream is sepia, colored in faded browns and reds like a vintage photograph. Movement in the dream is not fluid and smooth, but stuttered like thousands of tiny, barely perceptible adjustments. I see people. Sometimes they look familiar, but that may be an illusion of the dream. And these people shift. From one thing to another. Fat to lean, straight to hunched, shiny to ragged. Sometimes they shift from being to not being, completely vanishing in front of me. And sometimes the opposite, appearing out of nothing. Yet these shifts don't have the feeling of change–not of one thing transitioning to another, but more like one thing replacing another. A woman now. But then empty space.

Here was X, but now here is Y. Sometimes Y is similar to X, similar enough to know that X is what it's replacing. And with these shifts, these annihilations, these creations, there's no sense of destruction or pain or tragedy. It's just benign replacement. It all seems so fundamental to the nature of things, so much at the core of what's natural. And it isn't just people. Other things shift, too. I sense it, know it, more than I see it. The scale of shift can be colossal—cities appearing, forests vanishing. And it can be microscopic—an electron that flips its orientation.

And I know the dream will be gone when I wake up. No memory of it. I'll just need to wait until the next dream, tolerating my temporary illusions until I'm pulled back into reality.

SEVENTEEN

In Zhivov's kitchen, I suck on a melting popsicle which is all I have the stomach for. Too much to process, too much to rationalize. For example, there's acceleration technology available in 1996 that I knew nothing of a quarter of a century later. Asmus, an irritating prick for sure, but a ... time vandal? My mother and me and Tom laughing in the water sprinklers, oblivious to the feckless disease that will take her from us—*did* take her from us. And Prasad is so bloody secretive. I must be critical to his 'cure'; otherwise, why am I in the loop at all, if I can call this being in the loop? And why am I being hidden away in Zhivov's home?

Zhivov is out at the site right now and I'm alone. Prasad says I need to stay put. Gallie says I go nowhere without Zhivov. Zhivov tells me to not even think about leaving the house. All a good case for staying put. But the other side of that argument is *Fuck Them!* The keys to Zhivov's truck are right in front of me.

A car clutch is Satan's work, but I jog my way across town. What I'm looking for is the Big Red. It's not far from where there will one day be either a strip mall, or a park, or who knows the hell what.

I enter and it's dark inside, thick with cigarette smoke swirling under the dim, red-tinted ceiling lights. The wood-paneled bar is long and lined with high stools and brass foot rails. Behind it there are glass shelves of liquor with mirrors that double the bottle count. Only a couple of tables are occupied, each with a small candle lantern that doesn't threaten the anonymity of the drinkers. There are four or five men sitting at the bar looking at the baseball game and exchanging opinions. I sit at a table. The waitress, a young but worn woman in jeans and stained T-shirt takes my order.

I squint at the small TV screen as I sip my beer. It lasts me thirty minutes during which I contemplate how stupid my plan is. I stand to leave. And it's then that he walks in. I fall back into my seat. He walks with confidence to the bar without looking around him, sits and exchanges a few words with the bartender. Jesus, look at him. Dapper, slim, loose white open-necked shirt, pressed blue jeans and Docksiders. There sits the mighty manager of the Pacific Hardware South Risley Store. There sits my father.

He makes a joke with the bartender and the hunched, gray-hair sitting closest. I see him only in profile. His face is mine. Or would only *I* see that? It's the face I shave each day. The face that gave my mother the life she had. So, are you going to slug him? Is that the plan? To do something the ten year-old Joad couldn't? I wave over the waitress and order a second beer. He'll be dead in—I do the calculation—thirteen years. A shelf of cherry lumber will topple and he'll be right under it. A quick death. Nothing like my mother's.

On impulse, I take my beer and seat myself at the bar. There's no plan. Getting here was the only plan. He sips his beer and glances my way. He does a slow motion double take. We lock eyes for an instant but then there's a loud cheer from around the room and we look up at the TV. I keep watching the TV but sense eyes on me.

"This is Rodriguez's year," he says in a voice I'd

forgotten but now floods me with the familiar. I nod without looking. A pause. "Have you worked at Pacific Hardware?"

"No," I reply. I look directly at him. What do you see, Father? I realize that over the years my memory of him had adjusted to make him look more like me than he really did. He's no twin, but all the features are there and arranged the same. Hairline thin on the temples, jawline that juts, aquiline nose. And he must be about my age.

"I know you from somewhere," he says with the crooked smile I'd forgotten.

"It's a small town."

"Yeah, small town."

He looks down at his beer and I look at mine. From the corner of my eye I sense that he is now looking up at me but then looks back down at his beer. He does the same again. What to say?

"Shit week. Good to get away from it."

"That's what beer's for," he says. Now I sense him looking directly at me. "Nothing too serious, huh?"

"Well, is your wife fucking someone else serious?" He seems to be considering this.

"Depends if you like your wife, I guess," he replies with a grin.

"That's a solid point. Do you like *your* wife?" I ask. His smile fades.

"I do," he says and I nod.

"Do you fuck around on her?" I ask. He shifts on his chair to face me. It's not indignation in his face but bewilderment.

"What kind of question is that?" he says. I shrug.

"Want to hear about *my* wife?" He turns back to his drink.

"Sure, if you want to tell me."

"Her name's Bess. And the problem is I'm pretty sure she's seeing someone else. Do you know how that feels? It feels like absolute crap, every day, every minute. With me all the time." He stares at me. "At least we have no kids. That makes it better, right? Just one victim. Two if you count Bess." I point to order him another beer.

"Sorry to hear that."

I smile and keep smiling as I ask "would you ever cheat?" He stares at me.

"You sure we haven't met? You look real familiar."

"Well, give it some thought," I reply. "Maybe it'll come to you." He does seem to be giving it thought. Then he asks me about Bess, maybe showing some sympathetic interest in a sad drunk. So I tell him. How we met, how beautiful she was ... is ... will be. I tell him about the winery, about Den. How it all fell apart. I pretty much tell him our story. It lasts for a couple more beers. Then I ask him about his wife but he doesn't have much to say.

Our conversation wanes and we focus on our beers. What I want to shout into his face is *stop fucking around because your wife, my mom is desperately sad about what you're doing and you need to make the last five years of her life happy ones*. But I don't. Of course I don't. Then a petite, raven-haired woman in a flowing summer dress breezes up, puts an arm around him and kisses his cheek. He smiles awkwardly, more at me than at her.

"This is ..." he says to her, raising his hand in my direction. The pause is long.

"Joad," I say and smile at her. She beams back at me. I don't look at my father. She tells me her name but I don't hear it. Then there's the screech of chair legs on wood and I turn to see someone walking toward us. He's big, heavy, bald, yellow-bearded, dressed like a lumberjack, and there's violence in his face.

"Whore," he shouts, and without a pause swings for my father. It seems my father is fast and he steps backwards before the punch can land. Then he brings his foot up squarely between the lumberjack's legs who crumples to the ground, taking a chair with him. I look down at him as he struggles to catch a breath. My father has a useful skill for a man with the hobbies he has chosen.

I can't get caught up in this. I make for the door, hearing my father call my name above the rantings of the woman.

EIGHTEEN

The Big Red's parking lot is bathed in dull yellow light from the street lamp. I take out my keys but drop them and have to fumble under the truck's running board to find them. I recover them, squint to pick out the right key, and prod the lock with it until it enters.

"You!" I hear. I turn to see a figure approaching me. Oh no, this'll be the cuckhold's brother or friend. But then the figure extends an arm and I see a gun pointing at me, closing-in. *Oh shit. This is it.* The figure stops. It's a man, short, unkempt long hair, unshaven and looking as scared as me. He takes something out of his windjammer pocket. It looks like an iPhone. It takes me a second to digest that there are no iPhones on this calendar date. His face illuminates with whatever image he's looking at. "Would you be Joad Bevan?" he asks in a shaky voice. I look around me and there's no one. I hear the thud of music from a passing car.

"Who are you?" I ask.

"Shut up shag-bag." *Shag-bag?* It's an accent I can't place. British maybe. "Are you he?" I'm thinking the moment I say 'yes' will be my last.

"No," I say. "You have the wrong guy." He gets more

agitated and glances again at his iPhone.

"You *are*." He takes a step forward and the gun muzzle is a yard from my face. He's shaking.

"I'm not whoever you said. My name's Tom and I–".

"Y'are," he says. I squeeze my eyes shut. Then I wince with the boom of the shot and wait for my senses to catch up–the senses that tell me I'm hit and then dead. Nothing yet. I open my eyes. I look down. He's on the ground, his head in a pool of blood that's swelling over the tarmac. I squeal an exclamation as a hand grips my arm and pulls me hard. It takes me a second to absorb that it's Gerard Bruce, the red-faced TMA security guy.

"You're a prick," he says.

NINETEEN

"You're a prick," Zhivov says as he and Bruce escort me to my onsite quarters. I sit on my bed and hear a hushed conversation between them outside. Zhivov reappears but only to pull my door closed. I've been a naughty boy, I guess. Fuck them. Thinking *fuck them* somehow calms me a little. I'm shivering and I lie back on my unmade bed, pulling a blanket over myself. A man was shot through the head right in front of me and all I feel is numb and cold. I turn on my radio and Alanis Morrissette is singing "And life has a funny, funny way of helping you out." I shut down and drift off.

A knock awakens me. Gallie walks in, pinching two foam coffee cups with one hand and holding a bottle of liquor in the other. I sit up and come to, squinting in the light. She fills the cups and invites me to take one. I take a swig of Scotch and cough. She sits on my single chair. "You're not the only one who can break the rules," she says. I raise my cup to that. "How you doing soldier?"

"Oh, about how you'd expect." Now, Foxy Brown is inviting me to touch her, tease her, and I turn down the radio.

"What do you want to know?" Gallie asks.

"I want to know everything, Gallie. Everything." She nods.

"Yeah." She sips her whisky. "Of course." She's pondering something. Is it where to start. Is it *if* to start?

"How about, why did Prasad call me 'the awaited one.'? Let's start there."

"Because we knew you were coming. Well, we knew *someone* was coming."

"How?"

"Detected." *Detected?* "The Detection Array can detect arrivals as well as departures. You probably didn't know that."

"This is part of the inner-sanctum technology?" Gallie nods.

"When you accelerate, there's a whole bow wave of tachyons. They disperse over the timeline so we can guess when you'll be arriving—give or take a month." I'm impressed and I say it. "Same on the departure side. Enough of the tachyon burst goes up the timeline that we can detect a future departure. It's how we know where and to when your team was sent."

"Centuries away," I say. Gallie nods. That a guy from the future is learning about new technology is an irony I haven't missed.

"But that's small stuff." Gallie takes a sip. "All that's just about improved detection algorithms."

"So what's the big stuff?" I ask. Gallie takes a dramatic pause, or perhaps she's just catching her breath after an ambitious swig.

"Boris told you the mission space we're in. Preventing the one-second-per-second rule being broken is TMA's job, but our stealth business is remedying the fuck-ups when the rule *is* broken."

"Which calls for deliberate acceleration—for time travel," I say. She jabs her finger at me as confirmation. I pour us a second round. "You really do break the rules, don't you? I'm in the minor leagues for that, it seems."

"So, you'll be impressed by this. The newest accelerators can place you with an accuracy of seven minutes in a century." A spit take would have been justified but the whisky is too good to waste.

"So, a lot better than the piece of garbage accelerator that flung me back a quarter of a century when I all I was targeting was a couple of days."

"A lot. And there's another thing I think'll impress you," Gallie says. "An accelerator can now do temporal *and* spatial displacement."

I think through the implications through the fog of the whisky. "So you can wind up wherever, as well as whenever you want?"

"Accuracy of an inch in a hundred miles," Gallie says. I shake my head. "Ram was behind it all, of course," then adds in a whisper more to herself than to me "incredible man." I notice that I'm rocking fetally so I stop.

"So where are they? My team?" Gallie is up and raiding my food cupboard. She's happy with a large bag of potato chips and pops it open, grabbing a handful before throwing the bag at me.

"The silhouette portrait Boris showed you. Do you remember what—"

"I remember, yes." I posted her a *get on with it* look through my whisky haze.

"Well, you weren't the only awaited one. We detected another arrival a few days before you, but all we wound up finding at the arrival site was that portrait. No one with it."

"So someone's at large?"

Gallie shakes her head. "Not now." It takes me a few seconds of liquor-soaked befuddlement to think this through.

"The parking lot assassin." I say and Gallie nods. "Where was he from?"

"Don't know, but the portrait frame design turns out to

be American, late eighteenth century." Now I remember his language. Was that late eighteenth century? As if I'd know.

"That's where they are? My team?" Gallie nods.

"But why? Why eighteenth century? Why are they there? Who sent them?"

TWENTY

The whisky is going down too smoothly, too quickly. One pour follows another.

"The picture isn't clear," Gallie says. "But if you're asking for my opinion, your guy Kasper Asmus is a classic time vandal. And he's in the big leagues. I've never seen anyone trying to screw up the timeline on the scale I think he's going for." She takes another sip of the single malt. "Time vandals are usually jerks who've gotten their hands on the technology and decide to find out what mischief they can do. Go back, warn a friend off a future spouse. Bed a great-great-grandparent." I grimace. "Yeah, that one's sick, but common. One woman put a bullet into her husband's father before his sperm could cause her a problem." I chuckle. Can't help it. "A divorce of sorts, I suppose. Guy survived though. But the theory is, the timeline somehow has a way of healing itself, of getting back to the main flow. Perturbations tend to be short-lived. That's the theory at least."

"So the butterfly effect doesn't apply."

"Exactly. Where that theory lies on the spectrum

between incontrovertible and pure bullshit is open to debate. But even if it's valid, time does seem to have an elastic limit. Pull on it too hard and it snaps–like whatever caused your Risley park and vanishing wife."

"Snaps," I echo. "But what's a park in the scheme of things, I suppose? I doubt that'll change the big picture. Maybe it all settles down and the park was just part of the temporary perturbation."

"And your wife. Bess?"

"She was definitely a perturbation. Every fucking day." Gallie laughs and I do, too. "But then, so was I."

I hadn't seen Gallie laugh before. Not a real, convulsive laugh. Her face folds in on itself, her shoulders shake and she radiates.

"Anyhow," Gallie continues, "if we're right, Asmus is no petty time vandal. He's going for gold–a mass destruction of the timeline."

"But he'd be his own victim more likely than not, wouldn't he?"

"He's a psychopath. The power outweighs the risk for someone like him." She swirls the liquid in her cup.

"So what's he's doing? What nuclear-grade vandalism is he up to?" Gallie goes quiet. I sense she's giving pause to what she should tell me, maybe even regretting what she already had.

"A theory?" she says.

"I'll settle for a theory."

"We know where your team wound up. Late eighteenth century, Pennsylvania." Gallie looks for my reaction, which turns out to be a gormless stare. "Maybe just coincidence, but that time and place give the clue."

Even my thin knowledge of history yields a result. "The Revolutionary War?"

"If you wanted to shake things up just for the sake of shaking them up, you could do worse than mess with the founding of today's most powerful state."

"Shake up? How?"

"I'm balancing theory on top of more theory, but say you wanted a different outcome to that war. How would you do it?"

I ponder this and know my answer is banal. "Kill George Washington?"

"Maybe. But that'd take some luck. What we're thinking is that you'd load the dice."

"Load? How?" Now some of the dots start to connect themselves. "The bastard who was about to put a bullet in me. It was a semi-automatic handgun."

"Seriously asymmetric warfare, wouldn't you say?"

I shake my head. "You're kidding. That's crazy."

"Oh yes. Majorly crazy."

"You think Asmus is in the arms trafficking business?"

"Not so much a *business*. He'd be in it for the chaos, not the money." I lie back and close my eyes. The room threatens to rotate so I open them quickly. "This is all theory, Joad. We could be way off."

I wish I were sober to think this through. "And why kidnap the TMA team?"

"Don't know. Perhaps a cherry on the chaos—killing the capability to detect and stop accelerations. Maybe he just held a grudge."

"I believe that. I should have inserted some of his theory papers into his windpipe."

"And what his plans are, don't know. That's what we're going to find out."

"We?"

Gallie shrugs. "It's what you're here for, right?" I take a deep breath. There must be a hundred questions in me but they're drowned in fine single malt. I look at the wall clock and it's gone midnight.

"Don't you have a family to get home to?" I ask, bracing for seismic disappointment. Now is when I'm going to hear about the successful businessman husband and three beautiful kids in private school.

"I left my cat with a can opener. He'll be fine." Her head

is tilted and she's curling her hair around a finger in contemplation of something.

"Thank you." I say. "Thanks for telling me all this." She shrugs an *of course*. Bill Withers begins to lament that there *ain't no sunshine when she's gone* and I turn up the radio. "I dance to this. It's just what I do." I stand and begin to sway. Gallie stands looking like she's about to join me, but then lurches sideways and I catch her by the shoulders. Eyes lock for an instant then she pulls away.

She exits without ceremony and "need to lie down" are her trailing words.

TWENTY-ONE

I'm not built for hard liquor and never have been. And I only ever remember this when I'm hugging porcelain. It's a long night of thought, punctuated by unconsciousness, Saharan desiccation, and a nuclear headache. What Gallie told me seems insane even by recent standards. Loading the dice in the American Revolutionary War? Chronistically asymmetric warfare? A TMA team abducted to the eighteenth century? And Kasper Asmus behind it all? Is this really the most straightforward explanation of what's happened to me? If it is, what would be the far-fetched explanation?

The pounding inside my skull is not helping. So, is Asmus giving twenty-first century arms to British loyalists to change the outcome of the war? Goodbye US of A? A thought hits me as I lurch forward. Did his tampering cause the patriots to win? Is that it? Am I just like the kids in the Risley park who were oblivious to the fact that everything had changed? But for Kasper Asmus, we'd all be British. We all *were* British until he vandalized the timeline?

This doesn't seem like the place for analytical thought. Newton was sitting under an apple tree and Einstein in a patent office when they had their epiphanies. Not a single scientist I can think of was recorded as being draped over a toilet bowl during their eureka moment. I walk back to my cot and lie down with care.

No answers. No answers that don't double the number of questions. Gallie's laugh. Tom. My mother. Her husband. George Washington. Gallie's laugh. I pass out.

TWENTY-TWO

"C'mon, we're moving," I hear as I come to in a brutal jog. "Fifteen minutes," Zhivov says and vanishes. I walk dizzily to the sink, stopping midway to question the wisdom of even this short journey. I down a glass of water. Then another.

Zhivov returns when he said he would and I follow him out of the building, navigating the bustle of TMA cubicles. We get in his car and he pulls out while I'm still shutting the door. Exiting the parking lot, he takes a turn but in the wrong direction—away from the site gate. We drive for half an hour across the arid landscape that slopes down to the Columbia River, the morning sun flooding the land with pink and making the river glitter. There's a structure ahead of us shimmering in the sunlight. If it's there in 2021, I've never visited it. It's smaller than the TMA building, but otherwise made from the same trailer materials. We park and enter. Zhivov shows his credential to one of several guards sitting inside the entrance and we pass through a turnstile facing an open elevator. We go down. The elevator control panel acknowledges only two floors but the journey seems more like a skyscraper's worth. We must be getting as deep as the detection array. The door opens to a large, open space maybe a hundred yards square. The floor is a concrete pad and the ceiling is a hundred feet above us, crisscrossed by I-beams and cranes. In the center of the room is a large, cylindrical metal structure, maybe half the height of the room and fifty feet across. The room is lined with doors and Zhivov leads me to one of them.

The large, round conference table in the room is sparsely populated—Prasad, Bruce, three people I don't recognize, and Gallie. She and I exchange a glance. She looks luminescent, robust and well. I don't know how that's possible when I'm a gray, loosely bound bag of foul guts and pain.

"Given events, Dr. Bevan, time is of the essence," Prasad says. Is that a joke I wonder? No, this doesn't seem like the place for a joke. "It's only a matter of time before one of these attempts on your life is successful, so we should act. That's our thinking." He points to a chair and I sit. "This is Dr. Abioye," he says, nodding toward a woman maybe in her fifties with tight gray hair, dark skin and an expensive gray suit. "And Morales and Byrne, security." I nod and they stare. "Dr. Abioye has given us the go-head for a reconnaissance mission." Prasad doesn't explain who she is, but she looks like someone who's generally in charge, probably from D.C.

"Reconnaissance only," she says in a metered, soft voice, practiced to demand attention. "Not a rescue mission."

"Yes," Prasad agrees. "Right now we just need to understand the lay of the land. Find out where your colleagues are. What condition they're in. If they're captive. We're giving you four hours in the field to find out what you can. Maybe you won't find out enough to answer all those questions, or even any of them, but what we're going to do is send you to the coordinates your colleagues were sent to. That's no guarantee you'll find them of course, and if that's the case, so be it. This is a preliminary mission." I glance at Gallie who's looking down, arms folded.

"Mission team of four," Zhivov says. "Galois is team

lead. What she says, you do." I nod. "Bevan, you'll help identify anyone from your TMA team. Byrne and Morales are security."

"Do we know they're not dead?" I ask.

"No," Zhivov replies coldly.

"But I'd think it's easier to kill someone than accelerate them," Prasad says. "So let's be optimistic."

"They could be miles from wherever they touched down."

"Yes," says Zhivov.

"There are a lot of ways this mission could be useless, or worse, but it's where we start," Gallie says.

"Or worse?"

"Sure, " Zhivov says. "If whoever abducted your team is expecting us–if they detected the tachyon bow wave - they could have a nasty surprise in store.

"And we can't mask the arrival tachyon burst."

"No. We can shroud the departing acceleration blast, but not the arrival bow wave unless we happen to be arriving right in the middle of shielding facility," Zhivov answers. I nod toward the door.

"Is that what the thing out there is?" I ask. Zhivov nods.

"Can we communicate after we arrive?"

"With us? No."

"So, the first question is," Prasad says, "are you onboard with this?" My nausea has subsided, likely making way for the fear.

"Yes, I'm onboard," I reply. This took little thought. It's why I'm here, plus given how I feel, death will have no sting. Prasad nods at Zhivov who then slides matte charcoal gray boxes about six inches cubed along the table, saloon style, to each of the mission team. The top lid hinges open and I know what I'm seeing is an accelerator. It is very sleek compared to the jerry-built collection of components that had flung me here. A strap indicates it's intended to be worn like a watch so I put it on. A screen and touch pad curve around my wrist with what I assume to be the chemical and reaction chambers forming arm bracers like hoplite armor.

"You're a natural, Toad. Here's all you need to know about it," Zhivov says, pointing at my arm. "You won't be using it to accelerate out. We'll be using the main acceleration unit for that. What you need to know is that it's preset to accelerate you back here. Press the 'activate' key and you'll surf home on a wave of tachyons. Got it?" I nod. "If you're in doubt whether or not you need to use it, then you need to use it. And after you've been on the ground for four hours, it'll automatically activate and you're home."

"We got it," Gallie says, speaking for me. "We won't take risks." *We won't take risks? That'll be a trick.* I nod gravely.

TWENTY-THREE

So the fuse has been lit. I'm sitting on my hands for weeks, out of the loop, ignorant and frustrated, and now it's instantly decided that I'm to be blown out of a tachyon cannon right through the loop, and into god knows what on the other side.

"Been saving the best 'til last," Zhivov says. Aided by Bruce, he lifts a large cardboard box from the floor and drops it on the table. Bruce lifts the flaps and inside there's clothing. "Gotta fit in and not get noticed." He flings items at each of us. It's time to get all dressed-up, and Gallie leaves the room with what looks like an armful of rags.

Loose cotton shirt, a woolen waistcoat with a partial complement of buttons, breeches, stockings, leather shoes with buckles and a black tricorn hat. I struggle into them and Prasad rolls over a mirror. Good grief. Could be worse. Could be 1970s costume. Byrne and Morales look just as absurd. When Gallie returns, she's wearing a bulky, wrinkled brown dress that almost touches the floor. It's made of what looks like coarse wool, and over it is a white apron. A frilly white hat tied with pink ribbon is the finishing touch. We're not going as aristocrats it seems.

"A good look, all of you," Zhivov says. "But don't ask

to keep the clothes."

"Shut up, Boris," Prasad says. "So, to be clear, you have four hours on the ground. After that, your accelerator brings you home."

Bruce opens the meeting room door and adds "Or if there's even a whiff of danger, you press 'activate'. Got it?" We follow him into the cavernous space and toward the central cylinder.

"So what's our cover," I ask Gallie.

"Cover?"

"Our story. Who are we?"

Zhivov sniggers. "Well, you're a Prussian diplomat negotiating a lasting peace with the French. Your sister is a touring opera diva with the—"

"Dickhead," Gallie says. Our chortles stop as we enter the accelerator cylinder. I look up and around. The inner surface of the cylinder is lined with a metal mesh that extends over the domed roof, and I'm guessing runs under the concrete floor also.

"Tachyon absorber sleeve?" I ask.

Prasad nods. "Yes. We're very pleased with it. Virtually zero flux outside the cylinder."

Zhivov adds with a smile "And being tachyons, they're actually absorbed before they're emitted." Faster than light travel does have its quirks.

"How does it work?" I ask.

"The mesh is made of microtubes that circulate—" Zhivov begins to answer.

"There'll be time for that later," Prasad says. "Not a priority right now."

I see several tanks curving around the base of the cylinder which I assume to be super-sized chemical vessels and the reaction chamber. There are yellow concentric circles painted in the middle of the cylinder floor, from about a six foot to a twenty foot radius. The uneven, amateur paint job seems funnily at odds with the hyper-tech environment.

"Leatown, Pennsylvania is where we're going," Gallie says. "September 12, 1777. Should be daylight."

"And what will the arrival space be? Rural? Town?" I ask.

"No clue," Gallie replies. "Wherever it is, it's where your team landed."

"So maybe six feet underground in an airtight box?" I say.

"That would be a reason to hit 'activate'," Zhivov says. "Gallie, Toad, center circle. Back-to-back."

"Why back-to-back?" I ask.

"So if there's something to be seen," Gallie replies, "at least one of us will see it quickly." Morales and Byrne stand on the circumference of the next circle out, facing opposite directions and at right angles to us. They each take out a handgun, rack the slide, and hold it with both hands at arms' length. *Really?* Gallie pats my thigh. "You good?" she asks.

"I'm good."

Zhivov smiles. "Wish I were going with you."

"Good luck," Prasad says, then he, Zhivov and Abioye exit the cylinder. The door slams closed.

"The lighting will turn red," Gallie says, "then count five seconds and we're off."

TWENTY-FOUR

Several things happen almost simultaneously. I'm bathed in bright light, there's a volley of deafening explosions, I'm knocked off my feet by something heavy, and someone grabs my arm. I look down and see Morales' looking back at me, crumpled on my legs. Someone is pulling the accelerator off my arm, and the air is thick with acrid smoke. I see blood on my clothes but feel no pain. Maybe there's a delay and I'll be racked with agony any moment now. I look back and see Gallie is also laid out. I hear her voice but I can't tell what she's saying. We're surrounded by what seems like a dozen men in grimy, colonial garb, each carrying a musket.

"Up yer get," one of them says. "Yer alright." He pulls me to my feet. His teeth are black and he's unshaven with wisps of gray, greasy hair falling from his tricorn hat. I look over and see Gallie is being pulled to her feet. "It's a real pleasure to 'ave you 'ere," he says and his cohort laugh. "You as well, good lady." His accent seems more English than anything else. I look down and Morales is staring upwards, glassy-eyed. Byrne's face and chest are covered with blood and he's motionless. "Oh don't yer worry about them," the grimy man says, getting closer and misting me in his foul breath. "They were looking for trouble, weren't they?" he says, consulting his team. "We don't want no trouble 'ere." Gallie seems okay and no one prevents her from approaching me.

"You okay?" she asks.

"Yeah. Are you?"

"Yeah."

The chief goon grins at language he's not quite following as he puts our accelerators and the two semi-automatic handguns into a cloth sack. "And don't worry, we'll see to these two for yer," he says, nodding toward our fallen security team. Then the two men are lifted by their hands and feet and our assailants begin to walk away. Gallie and I just look at each other when we realize that we're simply being left. This is unexpected.

We find ourselves under a grove of trees in the gardens of large brick structure: too big to be called a house, too small for a full-on mansion, with half a dozen steps leading up to a grand portico bordered by Greek columns. Two dozen or more windows face us, including roof dormers and basement windows, all with white frames and shutters.

The cohort is maybe twenty yards away when the leader looks back. "See what yer find yonder," he calls, pointing to a wooden barn situated a hundred yards from the mansion. Gallie and I look at each other, and then, for want of a better idea, we set off toward it.

"They were expecting us."

"With some precision," Gallie replies. "Morales and Byrne didn't have a chance. They knew exactly where and when."

"Now what?"

"We stick to the mission."

"The mission didn't involve this. Not for Morales and Byrne, it didn't." I'm itching all over and take off my tricorn, grateful for the cool breeze. I try to take on board that half of our team was just shot to death. It's not real for me yet.

"Let's keep it together, Joad. We have a problem and

we'll work it through." So we have no route home, our security escorts are dead, and the best plan we have is to check out the contents of a barn on the advice of a band of thugs who assaulted us violently within less than a second of arriving. As we approach, I see two people in front of the barn who seem to be pumping water from a well. I squint.

"Those are jeans," Gallie says. We speed up. The wearers of the jeans see us and take a step backward, dropping their pail.

"Jenn?" I call. Then louder. "Jenn!" They walk tentatively toward us.

"Joad?" Her face is streaked with mud and her plaid shirt is ripped, hanging off her shoulder. She runs forward and hugs me, which is very much a first. The other figure is Arun Ramuhalli, a newly recruited tackychemist. I wonder how he's enjoying the job. "Are you here to take us back?" she asks.

"Not exactly. Not yet, at least," I say. Jenn looks at me, confused, and then at Gallie. I make introductions and Jenn reacts as if she's heard of Jane Galois.

"Are the others in the barn?" Gallie asks. Jenn nods. "Is it safe in there?"

TWENTY-FIVE

It's a barn from the outside and a barn from the inside, too. Daylight entering through uneven boards stripes the straw and the faces of the occupants. Some of the faces are looking down from a loft, others look asleep, and some are now directed at us. People begin to stand, descend the loft ladders and gradually cluster around us. Through grime, matted hair and unshaven faces I recognize Chen, McEwan, Jones, Wagner, Bisset, Alvarez, Kwame, Ito, Marlowe, ...

Gallie and I exchange a glance. "Is everyone alright?" Gallie asks. "Any injuries?"

"Alright? Bari, Holcombe and Huang are dead," Jenn replies in a whisper. "They took out our security team."

"Leaving just geeks and nerds," I say. "We're low risk, I guess." I look around and estimate maybe fifty faces. "More of you than I expected," I say.

"It's pretty much the full complement," Jenn says. "Both Washingtons cleaned out but for a few." I rest against a post to steady myself.

"How did it happen?" Gallie asks. Jenn shrugs. "It's like nothing actually *happened*. One instant I'm in the big chair. Next I'm tumbling on grass. Same with everyone. It all happened at the same time for each of us on the TMA site.

The others appeared seconds later."

"Kasper Asmus did this?" I ask. Confused looks are exchanged.

"He's not here," Ramuhalli says.

"What do you mean about Kasper Asmus?" Jenn asks.

"Is he behind this?" I say. I get only blank stares.

"Don't know why he's not here. Didn't know why you weren't here, either."

Gallie places her hand on my arm to say *let's stop with this line of questions.*

"Who's holding you prisoner here?" she asks.

"Prisoner?" Jenn says. "I wouldn't call us exactly prisoners. We can come and go whenever we like. But where would we go? There's a village called Leatown maybe a mile away so Andersen thought he'd do some reconnaissance. She points to a man with a red gash over his eye and a plaid shirt missing a sleeve. "Seems they didn't like the way he looked." He smiles sardonically and shakes his head.

"How long have you been here?"

"A month, but we're not tracking time well. Ironic, huh?"

"How are you surviving?" Gallie asks.

"They feed us. Every day. It's disgusting but they're keeping us alive."

"Who is?" Gallie asks. "Who's doing this?" Jenn shrugs.

"All we ever see are goons with muskets."

"Someone lives in that house," Ramuhalli says. "Never tried to get near it but I'm guessing if you did, you'd wind up with a lead ball in your belly."

I begin to notice the smell. It's stale food and stale human. I step back outside the barn and look across to the house. The musketeers are milling around it, talking, laughing and spitting. Jenn was right. These are goons and not disciplined soldiers. Ramuhalli follows me out.

"If I say 'arms trafficking' would you know what I'm talking about?" I say. He stares at me. "Are you seeing any modern weapons?" He looks bemused and shakes his head. It's looking like all our theories could be bullshit.

TWENTY-SIX

The food served to the barn-dwellers was not Michelin.
Two vats of bones and fat floating beneath a protective layer
of grease, with a barrel of turning apples to cleanse the
palate, all delivered by armed waiters so contemptuous that
even a Parisian restaurant would have fired them. *Tuck-in*, I
think I heard one of them say. *I ordered fries* someone had
shouted from the loft, safe in their anonymity, but it could
only have been McEwan because it wasn't me. Jenn had
handed me a tin bowl and spoon. I had declined.

Gallie and I return to the grove of trees under which
we'd appeared. "So, on a positive note," she says, "we
achieved our mission." Her smile isn't real.

"They were pretty useless," I say. "They don't have a
clue what's going on."

"Yup. I did expect more."

"And they're free to roam. Didn't you think they'd be
confined somehow?"

"They *are*. A time prison is pretty airtight. And if they do
summon the guts to wander off, they can only screw up the
timeline even more. A good strategy for a time vandal,

right?" We look at the mansion and the gaggle of guards surrounding it.

"I think the answers are in there," I say. Gallie pulls off her ribboned hat, her hair falls onto her shoulders, and she scratches her forehead.

"Even if the answers aren't in there," she says, "I'll be willing to bet that our accelerators are."

"I'm not a violent man," I say, "but what I'd give for one of those handguns right now."

"You'd go in blazing?" She's smirking. I motion *you have a better plan?*

"The town. Maybe we can learn something about who's in the house."

"Did you see Andersen?"

"He walked into eighteenth century Leatown wearing twenty-first century clothing, talking with a weird accent and saying God knows what. Hell, *I'd* beat him up." Gallie lifts her skirt, rips something, and coins fall to the ground. I raise my eyebrows.

"What else do you have in there?"

"You'll find out," she replies.

TWENTY-SEVEN

After sunset Gallie and I walk down the wagon-rutted track toward Leatown. Looking around us at the meadows and trees in the twilight we could be in any era, any year. A few buildings—maybe farmhouses—come into view. We walk on, cross a ridge and Leatown comes into view. It's a disappointment. Maybe I was expecting historic Williamsburg, but what I got was a ramshackle collection of small, slapdash buildings, positioned without logic and composed mainly of vertical wooden planks. There's one brick building that may be a church and there's no outside lighting other than what spills from windows onto the uneven, dusty ground. There are people walking between buildings, stopping to talk, laughing. A knot of soldiers in bright red uniforms and carrying muskets are standing around a water pump as one of them stoops to drink from it. The red makes them British if the movies are accurate. We pause to take a breath, then with the agreement of a glance, we descend the slope to the town. The details of our plan stop here, except for finding someone who can inform us and doing it without being maimed or killed.

A woman in a billowing, dirty white dress and tight bodice approaches us. "Hello darlin'. Haven't seen you before," she says to me through speckled teeth, ignoring Gallie. "You look like someone who could 'andle two of us, me cocksparrer." Gallie pulls me away.

"She did have a solid point," I say.

"Maybe you two can hook up later," she says and then nods toward one of the buildings. There are men gathered outside its open door, smoke is billowing from its windows, and it's where the singing is coming from. "An ale house? Looks to me like a good start. You ready for this?"

We walk over and slip sideways past the men in the doorway, smelling their beery breath and feeling their eyes burning laser-like into me. Inside it's a riot of smoke, smells, noise and sardine-packed humanity. Woman are circulating, squeezing through the throng to pour ale from stoneware pitchers into the awaiting tankards. The tables are packed with men shouting, laughing, puffing on pipes, breaking into song, and stopping only to guzzle. In the corner there's a table of British soldiers, of low rank I'd guess seeing their disheveled uniforms, who are laughing and shouting no less loudly than anyone else. Other than the servers, I can see maybe a handful of women in the entire place, probably colleagues of the lady we had just encountered. We find the one empty table and sit. A beer maiden walks up and surveys us with some suspicion. Are we doing something wrong?

"Two ales," I say and put coins on the table. She stares. *We're already busted*, I think. I guess no one says 'two ales' and puts coins on a table. That's a clear sign of a twenty-first century visitor is it? But then she picks up two of the coins, briefly disappears and returns to slam down two tankards in front of us. I take a mouthful and wince. Gallie is scanning the place and I look behind me. We're next to a table of rowdy young guys, each outshouting the other. Then the shouting mutates seamlessly into song.

A lusty young smith at his vice stood afiling
His hammer laid by but his forge still aglow
When to him a buxom young damsel came smiling ...

I don't know this song but I swing my tankard and mouth random words as if I do. Gallie grins. After a couple of verses, I feel I'm fitting in. I laugh when they laugh. I shout when they shout. I disapprove when they disapprove. Then in a moment of relative quiet the reveler closest to me leans in. *This is it*, I think.

"Ain't seen you before," he says. His skin is sun-browned and pocked, and his eyes are cold blue.

"No, visiting from Philadelphia," I reply. I try to affect a strange accent but this logic is flawed as there are many varieties of strange, and all probably strange to each other. Yet my answer seems to satisfy him.

"Ain't seen 'er neither," he says, looking at Gallie. I look at her as if that'll help prompt my memory. By then he has turned back to his mates to answer an insult. The singing starts again and I join in. Two more tankards are ordered and our coin pile shrinks. I learn he's a farmer. He learns I'm here selling supplies to the British garrison. At least that had been his guess and I had nodded. After a while Gallie gives me an imperative nod that means *get the fuck on with it*.

"The big house up the hill," I say to my new friend. "Who lives there?" He surveys me carefully.

"Why you askin' me?" he says.

"Just wondering," I say. "Thinking I could do some business there."

"That right?" he replies and turns away. Then he turns back. "You and yer hedge whore can move on. G'arn."

We don't dawdle. The fresh air feels light in my lungs and we put distance between ourselves and the ale house.

"Let's call it a night," I say to Gallie. "That went downhill fast."

"And I thought you were bonding there for a while," Gallie says, looking back as a wave of uproarious laughter comes from the building. We're setting out for the path that leads to the house when I hear *oi, wait*. We turn to see two men approaching us. One of them is my bar friend.

"Where yer goin'?" he asks. "We was just gettin' acquainted." This feels like a boatload of trouble. "Yer never introduced me to yer lady."

"That ain't no lady," the second man says without humor.

"Was just bein' polite." He looks at me. "Why don't yer go up to the old 'ouse and knock on the door? See 'oo lives there. Me and yer lady have some business meanwhile." He grins and promptly grabs Gallie by the breast. Before I can plan my next step, the blur of Gallie's fist has come into direct contact with the kid's face causing his head to snap back and his body to drop. The second goon looks down in shock then launches at Gallie, fist raised. I step in to intercept but he's fast and I take an electrically painful blow to the jaw. Then Gallie wraps an arm around his neck, jerking his face down to meet her upcoming knee. The first kid has gotten up by now and I deliver a full-force kick to his groin. He doubles up and collapses. I look back to the ale house and see there's a gaggle of men outside the door. I squint and I'm pretty sure they had been at the same table as these two.

With an unspoken consensus they charge at us. We run. Gallie hikes up her skirt and we make for the ridge. My hope is that they're too drunk to keep up. This hope is dashed when I look over my shoulder. They're shouting words I'm not understanding but there's no mistaking the sentiment. One of them catches up and tackles me to the ground. I look down just in time to see Gallie's foot connect with his nose. The others have slowed to a trot, confident of catching us, laughing and contemplating their prey.

Then I hear someone shout "get up" with authority. I turn to see two redcoats each with a flintlock rifle pointed at us. I get to my feet as does the kid who'd tackled me. I'm nursing my pulsating jaw and him his bloodied nose. "Unless one of you wants a new arse, I suggest you fuck off home." There's a belligerent hesitation from the young drunks. *"Now!"* the soldier bellows and they raise their rifles to take aim. Gallie and I turn to run up the slope, not stopping until there's forest between us and the town.

TWENTY-EIGHT

We fall to the ground panting. It's a gibbous moon and there's enough light to see Gallie's face creased in laughter.

"You're fucking demented," I say. "You enjoyed that."

"Yes and yes," she says. I laugh, too. I lean up on my elbow and touch my jaw lightly.

"You hurt? Let me see." She gets close and inspects my jaw. I feel her breath on my cheek. I look into the compassionate eyes examining me. Strands of hair resting on her forehead are fluttering in the evening breeze as she pulls closer for a better look. I see the laugh lines around her mouth. I wish I had the guts to ... She kisses me with warm lips and I kiss her back as we fall into the soft grass. I feel her hands pulling up my shirt, caressing my stomach. I run my hand up her leg, lifting her heavy dress to her thigh. Breeches have a lot of buttons and Gallie helps me, laughing. Then I roll onto her, kiss her on the mouth, and become lost in the starlight.

We lie watching leaves flit over the surface of the moon.

Gallie puts her lips to my ear. "We need to find another kind of foreplay." I smile. So there will be a next time. A

95

cool breeze rises and the trees rustle. I feel myself on the verge of sleep.

"We should go back," I say.

"Let's stay here a bit longer," Gallie replies. "I'm not ready for that smelly barn." I hold her hand and roll on my side toward her.

"Where did you learn to do all that?" I ask. "That was savage." She affects hurt and I chuckle. "Not that. The self defense." She smiles but doesn't answer. "Except that you have a cat, I don't know much about you, do I."

"I like it that way," she says and now *I* affect hurt. "Okay, what do you want to know?"

"Let's start with family. You know a hell of a lot about mine."

"Mom, mechanical engineer. Dad, chemical engineer."

"Ah, so you're from good diverse stock," I say. "Siblings?" She's quiet and it takes me a moment to see the smile has gone. "I'm prying, I know. There's plenty—"

"No, no, it's fine." She sits up. "Yes, a sister. Older sister." The pitch of her voice has dropped. "But she died."

"I'm sorry." I sit up, too.

"Long time ago." I know that I don't know what to say so I stay quiet. "Very smart she was. Smarter than me, I think. Still in high school." Gallie looks at me. "But she crossed paths with the wrong people one night."

"That's awful," I say, knowing how inadequate it sounds. She nods.

"Anyway, I'm not sure what comes next, but let's not risk going back to Leatown for a while."

I shift gears with her. "Might Prasad send a rescue team?"

"We didn't plan that, but yes, he might."

We sit for a while longer and I watch the moving shadows cast by the pale moonlight, listening to the sound of the rustling leaves. Then we dust ourselves down and head in silence toward the barn.

TWENTY-NINE

For a week I live the barn lifestyle with my friends. Funny that I now think of them as friends. It's far from how I thought of them on the site. But now we're huddling together in a frightening place, sharing the same incomprehensible risks and with an equal chance of surviving them. No schemes are hatched, no plans plotted, yet I'm asked constantly for assurances that we'll be rescued. I have no assurances to give, but I give them anyway. Jenn has become a *de facto* leader and is who they go to to resolve disputes, test ideas or proffer theories. She's cool under pressure and never loses her temper. This is why I would have never sat in the big chair. Yet, I figure out that she was obviously not part of the inner sanctum that knows about TMA's *other* mission. It seems to me that she's exactly the sort they should want on the inside, but TMA works in mysterious ways. Gallie has become Jenn's lieutenant. She has a way with words that Jenn does not and knows how to lay out the case for a decision that Jenn has jumped to intuitively.

And of course there's much coition going on. Whether those relationships had arrived with them, or whether it had just suddenly seemed like a good idea, who knows? The only rule was, use the back of the loft and keep it quiet. I once saw Mack McEwan try to make a move on Gallie. I don't know what she had said to him but his lumbering six foot four inch frame retreated with the bearing of a man castrated.

Hygiene is a mixed bag. Our host had thrown us a bag of toothbrushes, nicely wrapped twenty-first century-style and soap bars that looked like they had been collected from a chain of Marriotts. It's the little flourishes that count, I suppose. It's all too strange for a dream.

It's on the seventh night by my count that the bedraggled, armed goons march into the barn looking for someone. "You," the head goon barks, pointing at me. I do the looking behind me thing. "Yer must be quite the special one. The master has invited yer to dinner. And 'ee wants you to bring yer lady." *Lady?* Sounds like the 'master' has been tutoring him in manners. "We'll be back in an hour to take yer." He is as close to being courteous as he can bear, is the impression I get. Notwithstanding his polite invitation, his expression says *you might be in favor now, but I can wait. Then you'll see.* They slouch out and many conversations erupt simultaneously.

"I don't know, I don't know" I answer to questions from all directions. Gallie grabs my hand and leads me out of the barn. "Maybe we can get to the bottom of this," I say.

"Maybe, but that's not the way our luck's been going," Gallie replies and nods toward the big house. "I've no idea what's in there, but just keep your eyes open. Okay?"

"I will ... for what?"

"Anything. Danger. Something that might help us. Or kill us. Be nice if our accelerators are hanging on a coat rack. Just stay vigilant."

"Kill us?"

THIRTY

We're marched to the mansion portico. A young woman with black hair pulled into a tight bun and a black dress with white apron opens the door. Her eyes stay low but we're bidden to enter. Two of the guards enter with us, the others positioning themselves on the portico steps. The maid says nothing and we assume we're to follow her which takes us up a grand staircase, illuminated from above by a large, crystal candle-lit chandelier. Gallie and I exchange a glance. There are enough mirrors to derogate the Chateau de Versailles, and where there are gaps between the gilded mirrors and rococo sconces, there are paintings of lords leaning on swords and sheep grazing in meadows. From the outside, an eighteenth century mansion looks like a twenty-first century mansion, but when you're inside, there's no mistaking that you're not in Kansas any more. There's a dizzyingly wonderful smell of food and I hear a stomach rumble, maybe mine, maybe Gallie's.

We get to the landing. "The master thought you might wish to perform your ablutions before dinner," the maid says. She opens a door and invites Gallie to enter. Pleasant scents waft out, and peering inside I see a bathroom befitting the Versailles theme. Gallie enters without hesitation. So much for vigilance. One of the guards takes up the position of sentry and then I'm shown into the next room down. I enter Nirvana. There's a bath full of warm water, soap, scissors, folded towels, twenty-first century razors and an inventory of toiletries that'd shame Bed Bath & Beyond. Laid out is a fresh white linen shirt, breeches, waistcoat, jacket and, with disregard for the calendar, Fruit of the Loom underwear. This will take a while.

I emerge fresh and defouled and my guard pats me down. Then, despite menacing looks from the other sentry, I walk down and knock on Gallie's door. "You okay?" She calls out that she is, but not ready. After fifteen minutes she emerges and I mouth *wow!* She's wearing a floral dress that's somehow split in the front to reveal a white petticoat. I look upwards just to look away. *Why now?* I wonder. Why does the universe bring us together this way. Why not at a party or in a bar? Or in the grocery store, our hands touching as we reach for the same jar of pickles? Then I remember it's because the universe is an imbecile. That's why we both have a job in the first place.

"Sir, Ma'am, this way." The maid has appeared and beckons us to follow. "The master will receive you in the drawing room." We descend the staircase and turn into a large room lined with paintings—portraits, landscapes, frolicking lambs. Chairs, tables and couches I would normally think of as antique are positioned around the room, seemingly at random but I'm sure conforming to some classical style. "He'll be here shortly," says the maid who curtsies and promptly exits. We wait in silence for what seems like an age. Is the idea to increase the tension? If it is, it's not needed. I feel sweat on my palms.

A man decked out in eighteenth century silk and satin enters with a smile wider than his face. "Joad," says Kasper Asmus and he shakes my hand before I have a chance to consider withholding it. He looks more or less as he had looked when he tried to kill me in my Risley home, his eyes maybe even more sunken, his neck more ravaged by gravity, and with no signs of the beating I had given him.

"Kasper," I say, affecting nonchalance, "we were expecting you."

"Indeed? And may I have the honor of being introduced to this beautiful lady?"

"This is Jane Galois," I say.

"Ah, the famous Jane Galois," he says with a brisk bow. "I'm honored to have you in my little home—both of you."

I look around me. "Quite a place, Kasper. Seems out of the price range of a tackychemist, though." Asmus chortles and waves at a waiter in white wig who promptly brings us drinks in crystal glasses on a silver tray.

"English port. No better. It'll lubricate the path for a very fine meal Mrs. Asmus has chosen for us." We take our drinks and the waiter bows.

"It's very good," says Gallie. I know she'll have a sense of how to pace this, whereas I'd cannonball-in at the deep end with big questions.

"You've picked a nice time of year, no longer too hot and—, ah, my darling wife, Elizabeth," Asmus says. I look up from my drink and narrowly avoid a spit take when I see who it is. Bess, or her double. I look again to make sure I'm seeing what I think I'm seeing. There's no mistaking her. It's Bess. She's smiling at Gallie then turns to me. After a moment her smile fades into that look of embarrassment that goes with not recognizing someone you should.

"Hello," I say. She's not exactly the Bess I last saw. I'm no substitute for Carbon-14 dating but I'd guess she's maybe somewhere in her forties. Yet her porcelain beauty is undiminished. Asmus sees the discomfort.

"Oh really, you two. Of course you recognize each other. You were at college together." Bess's eyes open wide.

"Joad Bevan," she says. "I'm so sorry." She walks over and kisses my cheek. I glance at Gallie who's wearing a frozen smile. "It's so long ago." I agree with her and then force my gaze away.

"I'm famished," Asmus says. "I'll bet our guests are,

too." He beckons us to follow him. "You know, we could have laid on some fine eighteenth century fare like roasted partridge and turnips, but I thought you'd appreciate a good old steak and fries. Am I right? That sound good?" The words alone cause a cascade of digestive juices. We follow Bess into what must be the dining room. Paintings line the walls and in the room's center is a long dining table that could have accommodated two dozen guests, but is set at one end for four. We sit and food is served immediately by two white-wigged servants who spoon fries and meat from their platters onto our china plates.

"So, is the past what you expected?" Asmus asks and looks up from his steak for an answer.

"We've had a very limited view of it," replies Gallie. Asmus nods his understanding, deliberately missing her point. My own questions can wait until I've shoveled in a few more mouthfuls. Each time I momentarily look up from my eating frenzy Bess is staring at me. For a few minutes the only sound is the clattering of silver on china.

"Don't eat those plates. They're expensive," Asmus jokes and Bess smiles.

I put down my fork and take a deep breath. "What's going on Kasper?" I ask. He looks at me, affecting bafflement.

"Going on? We're just old friends sharing a meal, aren't we?"

"Some older than others," I say.

"Ouch," Asmus replies smiling at Bess. It seems like an instant ago that a Kasper Asmus was forcing his stupid papers at me to read, and it's getting harder for me to connect the two versions of him.

"Why are you here?" I ask. He ponders this.

"That's a good question. It's an interesting place in history, don't you think? Nice to have a first-hand view."

"Living in a chateau," Gallie adds. Asmus evaluates her.

"With the entire staff of TMA in your barn," I add. He raises a finger to a waiter who knows to pour wine, and then with a wave dismisses him. I look behind me to see two of his disheveled guards standing just outside the dining room door, not looking in our direction but obviously ready to act if needed.

"Know much about these times?" he asks.

"The Revolutionary War, you mean? I know the Americans won," I say. Asmus smiles.

"Yes. But being here right in the middle of it can change your perspectives a little," he says. He sips his wine and then compliments the waiter. "*You* might call it the Revolutionary War, but from here it looks rather different. Sitting right in the action, it just doesn't feel like a revolution. Not to me anyway."

"What does it feel like?" I ask.

"Like what it is: just another proxy war between the British and the French. Been going on for centuries."

"Interesting way of looking at it," Gallie says.

"But it's the way it is. Like you, I learned in school all about the uprising of the patriots to meet their destiny, but do you think the poor slobs down there in Leatown give a crap whether they're being governed by King George or by a Continental Congress? Nah. It's a handful of rich landowners who are the only real stakeholders, and they figure they'll get a better deal if they align with the French. And lucky for them, the British are about to be consumed by another war in Europe so the French are in with a shot here." Asmus sits back in his chair with the air of someone who's about to grace us with his wisdom. "You see, when you've been to the places I've been, you see there's a big, big distinction between the past and history. The past is just a collection of events that happened, that's all. You're both tackychemists so you get that. Whereas history is all about tales told by grayhairs—attempts to make stories out of the past, forcing the pieces together as if they have a plot and some kind of moral meaning. It's history that's the maker of heroes and villains, not the past."

Gallie smiles. "Thank you for dinner," she says and Bess

smiles back.

"Yes, dinner with friends is no place for politics," Asmus says. "Now, what would you say to hand-made ice cream?"

"Why are you murdering TMA security officers and imprisoning the rest?" I ask.

"Imprisoning?" Asmus says with indignation. "They're free to stay or to leave any time. As are you."

"They need to be free to go home."

"Ah. Go home." Asmus puts on a wide smile and sips more wine. "So tell me about your career with TMA Joad. Did you enjoy it? Was it fulfilling?"

"*Was* it? It's still going on unless you know different."

He turns to Gallie. "You see, Joad and I go way back. Old friends." I stay quiet. "It may be hard to believe looking at us now, but I always considered Joad as a sort of mentor. He was a decade older than me and had his feet well under the TMA table." His smile fades. "I was so proud to be part of TMA. We all were, right Joad?"

"It's a privilege," Gallie says.

"Yes, a privilege" Asmus agrees. "But it turns out that my love for TMA was unrequited." He turns to Bess. "That hurts."

"Maybe it was your personality," I say, and Gallie squeezes my leg hard under the table.

"Well, yes, that's a fair point," Asmus says. "But none of us were the warm, fuzzy type were we? God knows you weren't, Joad. You see, at least your contributions were admired, appreciated." His smile has now vanished. "You know, I developed the theoretical basis for enhancement of the tachyon reflection coefficient by almost twenty percent?"

"Yes," I reply but it's a lie. I don't remember much about anything Asmus did at TMA.

"Yes. Guess how much credit I got for that." I shrugged. "I wanted to be in the big chair. You knew that. To one day be in the big chair." He looks at Gallie. "You made it there. You know what that means to someone." She looks back at him but says nothing. "I got nowhere in TMA. Nowhere. And the people who did ..." He looks into middle distance. "Maybe I was no Prasad, but I was next tier down. I was. Is that arrogant? But I was. And it took me *nowhere!*" For an instant his face contorts, but just as quickly he regains his composure. "But *c'est la vie*. I'll call for ice cream."

"I don't want fucking ice cream Kasper. I want you to let us take the TMA team back." He looks offended.

"No ice cream?"

"Why did you take the 2021 team?" Gallie asks calmly. "You were just starting out then."

He nods. "Yes, good question Dr. Galois, I *was* just starting out. Yet, it had already set in. I knew I was going nowhere even then. Couldn't understand it." He looks at me. "It didn't take long for me to be the reject. The guy without a future." He takes another sip of wine. "So I decided one day, why not go back to the very beginning. That's the TMA that set my career in the direction it was always going to go. It was their doing."

"So you thought you'd just abduct them all and teach them a lesson?" I say. "And thought you might as well blow up the array while you were there. Remove some temporal protection, indulge in a little time vandalism." Asmus raises his palm upwards as if to say *will you listen to this guy?*

"That makes me sound like a lunatic." He grins. "And as you know, I didn't get *all* of them." I look behind me again and one of the guards looks back.

"So you and your goon came back to kill me just so you'd score the complete set."

"Well, I wouldn't put it that way. Besides, I knew you'd make trouble for me left to your own devices. And here you are, making trouble for me."

"So this is where you kill me?" I ask.

"What?" he feigns shock. "Why would I do that now that you're reunited with your friends? And certainly not before dessert." He picks up a bell and rings it.

"And the arms trafficking?" I ask. He leans back as a

bowl of ice cream is placed in front of him. He affects puzzlement.

"The what?"

"Giving them the weapons."

He speaks around a mouthful of his dessert. "Weapons? Hmm. Interesting concept. But now you're the one who sounds crazy." I stare at him but my curiosity is not reciprocated as he digs into his dish of ice cream.

"Dr. Galois, can I show you around the house?" Bess says. Asmus looks disquieted for a moment, but then his smile returns.

"Yes, of course," he says. "You'll enjoy a tour. Leave the menfolk to talk serious matters. This *is* the eighteenth century, after all."

Gallie forces a smile as she and Bess get up to leave and I'm left with Asmus. "It's pathetic," I say. Asmus raises his eyebrows. "So you went back and made sure Bess could never marry me. Teach me a lesson, eh? That's so very sad, Kasper. Sad even for you." He shakes his head.

"You're barking up the wrong tree there, Joad. That never happened. Besides, to be honest, you missed a bullet. She's a handful–fucked most of the British garrison." He belches.

"You really are an asshole Kasper."

"Keep the clothes, by the way. You look good in them. Your big chair whore, too. By the way, there's quite an age difference between you two. Must be like fucking your mother." He stretches. "But, you should be getting back to your team. I thought I'd let you be the one to tell them what's happening."

THIRTY-ONE

Fifty parents had waited up for us. We huddle in the dark of the barn while Gallie and I share what we've learned. The sheer incredulity that Kasper Asmus is behind all of this causes a dozen conversations to erupt. Then the volley of questions. Why this era? Why is he in a mansion? When will we go home? *Will* we go home?

"This is crazy," Ramuhalli says and jumps up. "*He's* crazy." Jenn takes his hand to pull him back down but he snatches it away and storms out of the barn.

"You have to feel for him," Jenn says. "Not what he expected out of his new job."

"This is not a problem suited for tackychemists," Gallie says. "*Crazy* isn't our specialty." We are asked more questions and give the answer *I don't know* in a hundred different ways. Then the talking wanes but for the occasional obscenity. I hear someone weeping in the dark.

I open my eyes to the daily chores that have already begun. Someone is raking hay across the barn floor. There's the clattering of tin trays being brought back from a rinsing at the well. I dwell on the fact that the serving of gruel could stop at any time. It's repulsive slop, but it's keeping us alive. For an instant I feel gratitude toward Asmus. Then that disgusts me. Gallie comes over to sit by me and is about to say something when Mack McEwan lumbers over.

"You have a visitor," he says, pointing to the back door of the barn. Gallie and I are nonplussed. I step outside and my visitor turns to face me, rubbing her upper arms in the cool morning air.

"Bess," I say. She smiles.

"No one calls me Bess." I apologize. "No, you can call me that. I like it."

"Okay ... well ... What can I ... sorry this feels awkward, Bess."

"I think I know why," she says. "At least I do if we're feeling awkward for the same reasons." The trees are casting a long shadow over us as the sun rises, and there's a cool breeze that isn't yet comfortable.

"Do you? It's just that, we do have a history, but I don't know ... which one it is." She waits for me to continue. I don't.

"Yes. No," she says to fill the silence. "That's sort of why I'm here. I do have a ... version of our history, Joad, but it's very short, simple. I know because of the weirdness that goes on around my husband that not everyone remembers things the same way. So I just wanted to tell you." I nod. "That okay?" I nod again. "Yesterday I didn't recognize you at first because it was so long ago. I hope I didn't seem ... rude." I'm looking at her and I'm seeing the wife with whom I could count in the thousands the times we've gone to bed together, shared private jokes, had intimate conversations, told her that I love her, and argued savagely. But our history is very short and simple, she says.

"Rude? No, not in the scheme of things."

"So this is it: You and I had one date in college. Just one. Met during Orientation Week, I think." *One date?* "Then I got a phone call." A smile flickers across her lips.

"A phone call."

"From your father." I must have look astonished. "So you didn't know? Yes, I don't know how he got my number, but he did."

"My father called you?" She nods and then hesitates, as if searching for the right words. It's a long search. "What he said to me was, and I remember this pretty exactly, because it's not something you'd forget. What he said to me was 'get the fuck away from my son or there'll be big trouble.'" I stare at her blankly.

"Oh."

"So, when you called me to ask for a second date, well—"

"Well, yes. Understandable." I'm staring at the ground because I can't look at Bess. "Indeed." My father was saving me. That's what he was doing. In his way. "So how did you end up with Asmus?"

"That was a long time and a marriage or two later. Met him in a bar in Albuquerque."

"And I never came up?" I ask. Does that question even make sense? Yes, sure it does if you're willing to bound across timelines. Or maybe it doesn't. I can't think.

"It would have been wild if you did. Those dots were never connected for me until yesterday. And even now, are they connected?"

"And he took you on a pretty wild ride, I'm guessing."

"Wild's the word," Bess replies. "One word, anyway." We're both looking for words when I notice a commotion coming from the barn—agitated voices getting louder. If Bess can hear it, she's ignoring it. "Now tell me your version, Joad."

Jenn bursts out of the barn door just long enough to say "need you," then disappears back in.

"Can you wait here?" I say. Bess grabs my hand and steps closer.

"I want to hear it—your version," she says, her eyes fixed on mine. I return her gaze momentarily then pull my hand free.

I overhear conversations and glean that someone has gone missing. Jenn, Gallie and Jim Chen are huddled and I join them.

"Arun Ramuhalli. He's missing," Jenn says.

"He's been taken?" I ask.

"Maybe, but I don't think so." Gallie nods at Jim Chen.

"Arun was hyper agitated last night," he says. "Kept getting up and pacing, muttering. I think he took it real badly ... what you told us about Asmus." Gallie and I exchange glances.

"So he's gone AWOL?" I ask.

Jenn looks at Chen. "For a while now he's had a theory," Jenn says. "A bit of a nuts one." She nods at Chen again.

"Yeah. He was sort of convinced that if you follow the wagon track in the opposite direction from Leatown you'll wind up in a city, or big town, or something."

"I think he thought twenty-first century Philadelphia is that way," Jenn adds. "Or something more civilized than Leatown, anyway."

"Based on what?"

"The wagons and coaches we see coming from there, I guess. It's not an airtight theory."

"So a bearded, Indian guy in twenty-first century clothes is walking up the wagon trail. Oh, he'll be fine. When did he go missing? Anyone see him this morning?" Heads shake. I stand and shout "did anyone see Ramuhalli leave? Anyone see him this morning?" No response. I sit back down and take a breath. "I'll look for him."

"Why you?" Chen asks. I lift my arms and look down at myself. "You're not the only one who can wear those clothes."

"You expect me to give up these fine threads? Besides, I'm clean and fed."

"I qualify too," Gallie says. "And I can take better care of myself."

"Well thanks for that, but I think someone is going to notice Jane Austen *en route* to the debutante ball."

Gallie grimaces. "Okay Darcy. You're it."

"Give me a minute." I exit the barn to look for Bess but she has gone.

THIRTY-TWO

Strangulation is at the heart of my plan once I catch up with Arun Ramuhalli. This is a man who survived the meticulous and excruciating scrutiny of the TMA screening process, and yet he'd do something as fabulously wild as running off into the night of an alien era. I imagine him lying in a pool of his own blood that's swelling with each dying heartbeat, and I picture a terrified young guy who could never have imagined his well-earned Ph.D. leading him there.

Setting out I have a sack containing a few supplies Gallie put together for me: a few bones and fat salvaged from the *haute cuisine* served to Asmus's barn guests and a cloth-covered jug of water. At most, this is two days' supply—one out and one back. I pick up the pace. To my right are open meadows so I'm likely to see trouble coming from way off, but on my left there's forest that could conceal a multitude of dangers.

I walk throughout the morning and then ahead of me the road plunges into the forest. My fantasies of strangulation sharpen. I enter the forest and the temperature drops as I walk through patches of light and shadow. Do I need to be worried about wild animals, too? I have the thought that for a tackychemist with expertise in temporal acceleration, I've never bothered to learn much about other times, about history. But then, my job was to block acceleration, not ride it.

I take a bone from my sack and gnaw the threads of meat off it. I spit. Then my thoughts drift to Bess. She looked different yet the same; strangely unburned by the fire of time. And I think about my father who did what he did. Saving me from her. As if saving my mother from himself? That'd be a profound thought for my father. In Bess I see a woman who is front and center in the last decade of my life and in my plans for the rest of it, and she sees a man who was a single night out, a few drinks and maybe an awkward goodnight kiss.

It's twilight and I need to turn back. Ramuhalli has sealed his own fate and I'm not going to kill myself over it. It's then that I hear a new sound and I dive off the road, rolling down the slope into the foliage. It had sounded like the whinny of a horse. I lie on my belly looking up the slope and wait. The horse appears, mounted by a soldier, then another, and another, all in single file. I count about ten horsemen, all uniformed in the blue of the Continental Army. Following them is their infantry, some in the blue, others in ragged civilian clothes, and all carrying rifles. There are maybe thirty or forty troops on foot. I freeze until they pass. They're headed to Leatown, is my guess, to give hell to the British garrison. Maybe give some to Asmus, too. That's a nice thought.

The cold thing on my ear is a bayonet. I don't risk moving my head but strain my eyes to look up.

"Stay as you are," a deep voice commands.

"What is this we have here?" This is a second, high-pitched voice. Then I'm grabbed by my collar and brought up to my knees. Both men are wearing grimy, ripped civilian clothes and pointing flintlock rifles at my face. The one with the bass voice pats me down for weapons, then opens my sack. The other keeps his musket trained on me.

"A tory spy is it?" the shorter one with the higher-pitched voice says. They both have an accent indistinguishable from those I'd heard in Leatown; sort of British yet different in a way I can't pinpoint.

"No, I'm not a spy," I say feebly.

"Ah, I'm pleased to hear that," the short one says. "Be on your way then." They laugh heartily.

I'm marched up the slope at gunpoint having gained the attention of the motley column of troops. Messages are being mumbled up the line and eventually the column comes to a halt. I'm walked to the head of it where a mounted soldier looks down to study me. His blue jacket is adorned with gold and his white breeches are spotless, tucked into shining black boots. He asks where they found me. The short soldier tells him. The officer scans the surrounding terrain and then looks up through the canopy of trees.

"We camp here," he says and dismounts.

I'm roped to a tree trunk, arms behind me. The soldiers settle down and gather in knots around campfires. On the other side of the encampment, a white marquee and a smaller tent had been erected, for the officers I assumed.

I know that spies being shot is a thing. They're probably not sure that I'm a spy though. But why take the risk? Yet, here I am, still breathing. The horrifying thought hits me that I'm alive only because they want to extract intel about the Leatown garrison. What do I know about it? Almost nothing. I'll tell them that. Yes, that's what I'll do. For a moment there, I thought maybe I was in trouble.

An hour passes and I see two soldiers coming my way. This is it. This is the end. I'm untied and marched across the camp under the surveillance of many suspicious eyes. Sitting outside the marquee and warming his hand at a campfire is the soldier—the general maybe—who'd led the column.

Besides him is another soldier, similarly dressed in blue and gold. I stand facing them through flickering flames with the two guards behind me.

"Your name?" the general asks. No point in making one up, so I tell him. "And where are you from?" That's a tougher one to answer honestly.

"Leatown," I say. The general takes a draft from a metal mug. In the flickering light of the fire I see his skin is pink and pocked, and his black hair is tied back over his ears into a low ponytail.

"Leatown. And what's your work in Leatown?" He's looking into the fire rather than at me.

"I'm a farmer," I say, because this is my first random thought. The general looks up at the other officer seated at the fire.

"He's a farmer," the general says.

"Indeed," the other one says. "He looks to me to be veh'y well-dressed for a farmer." It's a French accent. The general smiles.

"What do you farm?" the general asks. This may be where my entire story collapses because I've no idea what gets farmed here, now or two hundred years from now. All that enters the vacuum of my mind is what I knew to be farmed in twenty-first century eastern Washington state.

"Alfalfa." They look at each other bemused. "And wheat," I add promptly. Surely that's a safe choice. I should have said that first. The fire spits a cinder that lands by my foot. "Look, I'm just on my way home and don't mean to inconvenience you." They smile.

"You're no inconvenience Mr. Bevan," the general says. "Not as long as we have you as our guest. But I must ask you, from where are you returning?"

From where am I returning? Where *is* there to return from? I've no clue where I am. "My son," I say. "He ran off and I'm trying to track him." I learned from Bess—my version of Bess—that staying close to the truth is the best way to lie. This gets no response. They either bought it or they think it's too ludicrous to take the bother of questioning.

"Tell me about the Leatown garrison. How many British?"

"I don't know," I say. "I have no business with them." The French man chortles.

"I see. So your home is in Leatown, you're a farmer, but you have no dealings with the garrison?" the general says to the fire. He shakes his head. I sense my luck is taking a bad turn. Then a soldier walks up, stands stiffly to attention and hands a note to the pocked general. He unties and unfolds it, and leans in toward the fire to read it. He looks up at me. "We'll have plenty of time to converse more Mr. Bevan. I'm afraid I have more pressing matters at this moment."

THIRTY-THREE

I'm sitting tethered to the tree. The wind is picking up and the rustle of the forest is getting louder. On the microscopically small chance that I escape this, Prasad needs to be told that a little preparation for these trips would be a good idea. Dragging a hungover guy out of bed and then catapulting him across more than two centuries without educating him on where he's going is, put politely, a fucking stupid strategy. Knowing crops would have been invaluable. Yet, not a minute on crops.

From the fading chatter I can tell the soldiers are settling in for the night. Only one of them is close to me and he's lying with his hand on his musket. He rolls over and it takes me a moment to notice that he's watching me. He looks like a child, maybe fourteen years old at most. At first he seems to be shivering, but I soon realize that it's a tremble. He's terrified.

"You okay bro?" I say to him expressing genuine empathy but in a vernacular that was only for my own benefit. He doesn't move and just keeps staring at me, head on the ground. "Is this your first time?" I ask. "First time into battle?" I think I hear him say 'yes' above the rustling of the trees but his lips hadn't moved. "I've never been in

S. D. Unwin

battle," I say. "Must be scary." The boys sits up and looks around to see if we're being watched.

"Are you a tory?" he asks, hesitantly.

"Me? No, I'm no tory."

"Then why you tied up?"

"Well, it's just a misunderstanding between me and the general. I think he'll let me go once we clear it up."

"So you a patriot?" he asks.

"Yes, I'm an American patriot. Are you?" He looks at me, first with shock and then suspicion.

"'Course I am. That's why I'm here." He has stopped shaking.

"Where are you from?"

"Philadelphia."

"What job do you do there?"

"Work with my father. He's a cobbler."

"He a good father?" I ask. The boy says nothing at first and just rocks back and forth.

"He is."

"Good," I say. He tells me about his three brothers, two of them killed in battle. About his mother who used to work with his father but is now too sick, and about his sister who died in childbirth. I tell him a few things about my brother and parents, taking some liberties with place and time. Then a sentry walks by, looking at us both threateningly and the boy lies down, turning his back to me. The wind continues to pick up and I shiver.

I awake to frenetic activity all around me. I breathe mist into the cold morning air watching soldiers going through the labor of loading their rifles: pouring powder down the barrel, wrapping and ramming down a lead ball, cocking the gun, then pouring in more powder somewhere near the trigger. My young friend is doing the same, but struggling with it. "Hey, hey. What's happening?" I ask him in a loud whisper. He looks around.

"Redcoats comin'." I pull at my ropes but without hope. "We're going to ambush them." After he's satisfied with his task of loading his musket, my friend follows the other soldiers who are running down the slope and into the trees toward the road. Without warning, someone tugs my head back and then shoves something into my mouth. I'm being gagged.

"You so much as squeak and I'll blow lead right through you," says a deep voice I recognize. "Understand that?" I nod vigorously and he runs off. Now there's quiet. All I see are the trees and all I hear is my own heartbeat. I peer into the forest for what feels like an eternity. There's nothing. No motion, no sounds. Then a single gunshot, followed by a volley. That sounded like enough shots to take out a good number of redcoats. There's a moment's silence and I hear more shots. But these ones sound different. They are uncountably fast, almost continuous, and sharper with less of a boom. They coalesce into a solid wall of noise that lasts maybe ten seconds. A few moments pass and then soldiers burst out from the trees running through the camp, shouting words at each other I can't make out. These are the colonial troops beating a frenzied retreat. The general is among them yelling orders but I'm not sure anyone is listening. Some of the troops are stopping, beginning to load their rifles. Powder down the barrel, wrapping the lead ball, sliding the ramrod, charging the–. Then from the trees appear the redcoats. But these soldiers are walking with a demeanor approaching the casual, side by side, maintaining a line with a few feet between them. I count six, and each raises his gun, opening fire on the retreating troops. The guns produce not single shots, but bursts of fire and the retreating troops begin to fall in waves. One has managed to reload his musket and gets off a futile shot before his chest blossoms under a hail of bullets. My young friend emerges for the trees, staggering, one of his arms no more than red gristle. He looks at me with an expression not of fear or pain, but of confusion. Then with a burst of gunfire, his head ejects a splash of red.

I turn ice cold and can barely catch my breath. For the next minute I hear intermittent, isolated bursts of fire, and finally quiet. The camp is strewn with bodies, some intact, others dismembered. The redcoats, now maybe ten of them at most, walk among the bodies, exchanging inaudible words, occasionally laughing. I hope to god I go unnoticed but I know that won't happen. Eventually, one of them looks directly at me.

He approaches me, stepping over bodies and body parts. "Well, what have we 'ere?" he says. His uniform is disheveled, torn and blood-splattered. He's carrying what looks to me like an assault rifle: twenty-first century for sure. I'm no gun enthusiast but I can look at the bullet magazine, the grip and the sleek, black design and know that that obscene machine has nothing to do with the eighteenth century. That bastard Asmus had lied and Prasad was right. The redcoat pulls my gag off roughly and I check my teeth with my tongue as if a loose tooth would be a problem right now. " 'Oo ah yer, then?" I try to stop shaking and I tell him my name. He calls another soldier over, maybe an officer although no less tattered and scruffy. They talk in hushed tones and then, hands still tied, I'm shoved in the direction of the road, navigating the corpses strewn in front of me.

THIRTY-FOUR

I'm tethered to a cart for the march toward Leatown. The pace is rapid and I struggle not to fall and be dragged. After a few hours we exit the forest and eventually march past the barn and mansion, but there's no one to be seen except the goons milling around the mansion portico. We continue on through the center of the town and then through the tall gate of the army camp which has been opened for us. I'm thrown into a cell lit only by sunlight leaking through wooden slats. Furnishings comprise of a pile of straw in the corner. I'm untied and I rub the blood back into my wrists as I hear the clunk of the door lock.

What could Asmus's plan possibly be? Only sheer vandalism makes sense. Shaking it up. Exerting power just because you have it. In trying to understand the temporal logistics of what Asmus has done, my reasoning forms circles that eventually spiral into a singularity of logic. There's no sense, no predictability, no rationality to it.

After what seems like several hours, a tray is slid through a slot at the bottom of the cell door. It's water, dry bread and an apple, and I devour it all. Another hour passes and then the door bursts open. A guard steps in, stands to attention, and what looks like a British officer passes him without acknowledgment. He's wearing a white wig, has a look that parodies self-importance, and is not concealing his contempt for the things his job calls for.

"Name?"

"Joad Bevan."

"Why were you with the rebel army?"

"They captured me." I would have thought that being bound to a tree was a clue, but he looked like he wasn't about to fall for that.

"Where are you from?"

"Leatown," I say.

"Who can vouch for you?" he asks. I wasn't expecting this question. I didn't know what question I *was* expecting, but whatever it was, I knew it'd be my downfall. I hesitate. Am I really going to say this? What option do I have?

"Kasper Asmus," I say. This seems to give my interrogator pause. He scrutinizes me.

"Kasper Asmus," he echoes. I take it that this name carries weight. He seems fazed, so I run with it.

"Yes, I work for Kasper Asmus. Please tell him you've found me. I think he'll be grateful." I think no such thing. The bastard will probably disown me or worse. The officer says nothing, turns, and exits the cell followed by the guard. There's the heavy clunk of the lock and I rest back on the straw to wait, gnawing on a bare apple core.

He looks twenty five years old at most and is well turned out. The shirt is clean, the boots shine and his white, lace cravat is neatly-tied. I stand, which alerts the guard who takes a step forward. The young toff waves the guard away.

"United States president in 2020?" he says. I answer him correctly. "Only record in the 1990s to stay at number one in the country music charts for ten weeks?" He looks at me expectantly, then laughs. "Kiddin' ya." I manage a grin. He pats my arm. "Ya red pat?" I don't understand him. "C'mon old man. You don't speak mid-21st verno?"

I shake my head. "That where you're from?" I ask. Without replying he beckons me to follow him.

We exit the brig as guards look on deferentially. He has me sit next to him in the box seat of a wagon, and with a flick of the reins we're on our way. I look at him side-on and I'm in no doubt that he was, or maybe still is, TMA. I know because TMA arrogance radiates from him. Maybe it's his posture, or maybe his obvious comfort in ignoring me, but I have an immediate sense of him. It makes me remember my surprise at the collegial atmosphere of TMA-1996 compared to the egregious smartassedness of TMA-2021. Extrapolating that trend, mid twenty-first century TMA must be staffed by egos of planetary scale. It makes sense. On the other hand, this guy could just be a self-made prick. Whichever way, he's not answering questions.

It's a bumpy ride and I need to hold tight onto the box seat. You don't get a sense of the unevenness of the road until you travel it on wooden wheels with every shock, every jog shooting directly up through your ass. I try to figure out the timelines. Asmus was a toad of a man even at the peak of his appearance, so it's tough to figure his age. No younger than his 50s. So that'd put him around 2050 if he'd kept to his timeline. That's consistent with this arrogant little shit using mid-21st vernacular if he brought him back with him. But Bess started out a decade older than Asmus and there's no way that the Bess in the house up the hill is sixty something. Sure, older than the Bess that had vanished on me, but not by *that* much. So that means Asmus picked her up while time hopping. How uproariously funny it must have seemed in his barking madness to grab the once and would-be wife of the one guy who got away. What a nice setup for my comeuppance.

I want to see Gallie. She's been the only point of quiet for me in a tornado of lunacy. I need to see Gallie. Maybe we're en route to the TMA barn. But maybe not. No point asking this schmuck. I look him over and I'm pretty sure I could take him. But then what? The worst kind of prison is one without boundaries.

THIRTY-FIVE

We pull up at the service entrance to the house where we're met by two guards. They're carrying semi-automatic assault weapons. It seems the charade—the denial—is over. I yearn to be back at the barn, but instead, here I am at Chateau Crazy. With a sharp flick of the head I'm ordered to follow the guards. I know these could be my last moments alive yet I seem to be deadened to the worry. It could be terror fatigue.

I'm pushed into the drawing room and followed by my escort. The guards wait outside. Asmus is seated in plush comfort and Bess is standing by his side. Her left eye is black and there's a cut on her cheek. I look at Asmus with contempt, jaws clenched. Bess shakes her head almost imperceptibly to say *don't*.

"What an aggravating tackychemist you're turning out to be," Asmus says. "And stupid, too. I mean, imagine just setting off for a stroll in the woods when you're centuries from home. That *is* stupid isn't it?"

"You *are* selling arms, you mad fuck," I say.

Asmus exaggerates the taking of offense. "You speak like that to a man who just sprung you from the brig?" He looks at Bess as if seeking concurrence. "Add ingratitude to the list. Oh, by the way, did Mancini introduce himself?"

I turn to see a man affecting stony professionalism. "Meet Phil Mancini."

"Today I saw fewer than a dozen men slaughter a platoon in seconds," I say.

"It really shouldn't have taken that many men; not with the weapons I've given them. You see, it's about training. I can equip them with the best arms to be had, but at the end of the day, they need to know what they're doing with them. They need to perform like professionals."

"Why?" I ask. "Why do this?" Asmus sits back in his chair and I notice Bess wince as he takes her hand.

"Do what? Help kill soldiers? Isn't that what they're trying to do to each other anyway? Don't try to make out that that's my doing. And when you're dead, do you really care if it's a lead ball or a steel bullet that got the job done?"

"Killing a dozen humans in one burst of fire isn't the same as a 50/50 chance of killing one with a musket shot."

"You always were a second-rate mathematician, Joad. Don't you see that these weapons will accelerate the war to an outcome? And I'm pretty sure that that'd reduce the total death count in the end. Besides, where's your sense of humor? Isn't it a delicious irony that 2nd Amendment rights are what allowed me to get my hands on these weapons, and now they're being used by British troops to massacre a well-armed militia? Joyous, no? Come on, give me a smile at least."

"Yeah, joyous, Kasper."

"And I have other jokes to try out. All this is no more than a test run. Imagine the possibilities—the scenarios. Savage Vikings arriving on the shores of England all ready to slaughter the monks or whoever the hell they slaughtered, and what happens instead is that they walk into a mist of steel, blossoming into geysers of red and gore. Or the mighty Mongols descending on some defenseless village ready to serve up their brutal reign of terror and instead they find themselves up against the blast wave of a 50,000 kiloton nuclear device." There's glee in his face. "I mean, just how humorless would you have to be not to see the funny side of that?" He waves his hands. "Run away! Run away! Ha." I look behind me and see that his creature Mancini was unable to suppress a smile. "See what real power is?"

"And that's your plan?"

"Plan is a strong word. It'll be more of a whim if I get around to doing it." He looks up at Bess. "I'm prone to whims, am I not, Elizabeth?" She glances up at me. I sense that assaulting my TMA values is as much a part of his intent as massacring Vikings. This line of conversation will go nowhere.

"When will you set the TMAers free?" I ask.

"As I told you before, they're already free to leave any time."

"Give us back the accelerators."

"Well, that's quite an ask, Joad."

"You're feeding them mush, you bastard. Some of them are getting sick. They need medical attention. It's only a matter of time before someone dies."

"So dramatic."

"What have they really done to you, Kasper? Abducting the entire TMA team seems like an overreaction to the innocent consensus among them that you're a worthless little prick. Deep down, you can't argue with that," I say. Asmus's eyes open wide with rage, but he quickly regains his composure and smiles. Why the hell did I say that, just for a moment's gratification? I'm just pleased that Gallie didn't see it.

"Is there a reason I shouldn't kill you?" he asks.

"That'd be murder, Kasper."

"No, that's a legal reason. I mean a moral reason." I hear Mancini chortle behind me. "What am I to do with you?"

"Send me home. Send us all home."

Asmus affects to weigh this up. "Joad, what have you achieved in your life?" He puts on a concerned, paternal look. "I mean, you sit in the middle of nowhere waiting for some poor bastard in Seoul to haplessly make the wrong chemical cocktail and then you reflect a few tachyons to shut it down. That's it. Hell, you don't even do that. You do theory. Theory that might increase the efficiency of detection by a percentage point or two. Doesn't it strike you that what you do is utterly insignificant?"

"It doesn't."

"No?"

"You're a Tardis full of shit, Kasper." He shakes his head and again looks up at Bess as if expecting her to defend him. She glances at him and then at me. I can tell she wants this to end with me intact and I'm not helping.

"You know Joad, you might not like me or what I'm doing, but you can't deny that I'm significant." He looks up at the ceiling. "There are, what, a hundred billion stars in the galaxy, and who knows how many planets? And it's pretty likely this is the only one of those planets with life—at least intelligent life. So if you're going to have influence, then this is the place to have it. And what better way than to own the timeline. Be master of it. Tie it up into bows of your own design."

"Your own design? You have no design. You're just wreaking havoc that you can't control. You're a vandal, that's all. And that's what you call 'influence'?"

Asmus ponders this and then stands. "I shouldn't do this, but you do tend to make me do silly things. Come with me." He exits the room and Mancini shoves me to follow. The two guards bring up the rear, sporting breeches and assault rifles. He leads us through a door under the grand staircase on the other side of which is a long, thin hallway that ends at another door. We walk down it single file and as he faces the far door I hear it unlock—some kind of biometric mechanism I assume although there's no scanner in sight. We follow him inside.

It's the height of anachronisms. The furniture is Georgian: plush chairs and mahogany tables strewn around the room, the wall lined with fine art—portraits of white-wigged men and rosy-cheeked women, landscapes of meadows and brooks. But this room is not lit by flame. I see a black cubic unit in the corner of the room that's humming, likely an electrical generator: maybe a micro-reactor. The cylinder against the far wall, set between portraits of be-wigged generals, I'd guess to be a tachyon shield, maybe containing an accelerator and arrival area. It's ten feet in diameter and about as tall. Two slovenly eighteenth century goons are lifting a crate out of it. My guess is that it's full of twenty-first century arms. They place the crate on what looks like an oversized dumbwaiter and it descends from view. In the middle of the room is a baroque table at which a small woman with short, spiky red hair is sitting. Her clothing is twenty-first century and over her eyes she's wearing something that looks like a more compact version of a virtual reality headset. Her table is bare and seemingly redundant. Asmus looks at me for a reaction and I resist giving him the satisfaction.

"Control rooms, big chairs, monitors, analysis stations, accelerator facilities, staff of twenty," says Asmus with a smirk. "None of that. This room and one operator equals and exceeds the capability of all that, and the art is a nice bonus isn't it? Exadata analysis algorithms you never dreamed of, my friend. I'd try to explain some of it to you but you never did have time for that, so why start now? By the way, we're sitting on a tachyon detection array less than a thousandth the area of your TMA's yet with double its T1 detection accuracy score." I raise my eyebrows despite myself. "Yes, indeed," he says. "Not all my ingenuity I admit. I had mid twenty-first century tackychemical technologies to draw on, but then I made all this happen, with a little help from my friends." Mancini smiles toadishly. "Right here in 1777."

"You're pretty proud, huh?" I say.

"Proud? Sure, why not Joad? But how would *you* recognize something to be proud of? You have no experience of that, you see."

It occurs to me that being shown all this is a prelude to being killed. He'd only take the risk if it were moot. But then, maybe he thinks my being stuck here is as effective as being dead. The goons reopen the tachyon shield and remove another crate.

"Anyway, you caught me on a busy day, Joad. I'll let you get back to your team."

THIRTY-SIX

I'm left to walk back to the barn. The thought of seeing Gallie is the helium that lifts my mood.

I enter to what, by TMA standards, is chaos. From a knot of people there comes shouting and they seem to be vying for position. I part the throng with sheer brute force and what I find at its center is Gallie holding two men apart. Don Marlowe and Hugh Wagner are red-faced and yelling incoherently at each other.

"Enough!" Gallie shouts louder than both of them. "If you wanna fight then fight with me." There's a ferocity in her voice that scares even me. I suddenly see a younger sister who'll now take nothing off the table. But Wagner is dumb enough to push forward. "I mean it. You testing me? Are you?" She's facing away from me and her fine couture is now crushed like an old handkerchief and layered in straw. The two men each take a step backwards. "Wise. Listen to me: If this happens one more time ..." The threat is left unfinished. The two men walk toward opposite corners of the barn. Gallie turns and it takes a moment for her to register me. Then everyone turns, including Arun Ramuhalli and I glower at him.

"We need to talk," I say to Gallie and escort her out of

the back door, navigating people who are throwing questions at me. Once out, I shut the door and walk Gallie backwards until she's crushed between me and the barn wall. I kiss her, my palm on her cheek, and she kisses me back just as hard. I pull back and look at her. There are no words for a while. Then she leans forward to kiss me again, this time less urgently. I walk her away to put a few trees between us and the barn.

"What was all that?" I ask.

"Just Marlowe and Wagner being jackasses," she says. "The tension's getting worse. It was bound to happen."

"Let them fight it out. No point you getting hurt."

"By Wagner and Marlowe?" she asks? I smile. Then I give her a download—everything that happened. The weapons, the massacre, the jail, the accelerator facility. "Horrific, but I'm not too surprised, Joad. Prasad's rarely wrong."

"Yeah, he called it," I say. "So Ramuhalli showed up?"

"Uh huh. He never took to the road. He was just out having introspective thoughts in the woods."

"That may be another fight you'll need to break up. Little prick." I hear the voices of TMAers looking for us, speculating on our whereabouts. "What's Prasad thinking? Why has there been no rescue mission?"

"I never know what Prasad's thinking. That's a pretty unique brain he has there. One thing that occurs to me is that we each had an accelerator pre-set to return us after four hours. So either Asmus undid that preset, or they did activate and all that arrived at TMA was the accelerators with no bodies attached. Either way, Prasad must have known there was trouble. So what would he do? If two security guys did us no good, then would he think his main option was to send a bigger security team?"

"Maybe."

"But as you know, accelerating people *en masse* is a dangerous proposition. Something in the timeline is bound to get screwed up by that."

"But we've already got a barnful of TMAers here."

"Yeah. But the argument still holds doesn't it? The more people out of time, the bigger the risk. Truth is, we didn't have much of a plan. We just wanted to get the reconnaissance done and *then* draw up the plan. I see how that thinking was flawed."

"Ha. The great Prasad."

"He was trying to get you out of danger," Gallie says.

"So, on a scale of 1-to-10, how well would you say that worked?" She smiles. Within minutes we're found and escorted back to the barn for what I expect to be an intense townhall meeting.

THIRTY-SEVEN

Barn life drags on. Health deteriorates. Any pharmaceuticals that were being taken before the abduction had been left behind or had run out, and there is no way of treating new ailments. Chrissie Kim is in the worst shape, doubled-up in pain when it gets really bad, whatever it is. Fights break out more often and Mack McEwan has taken to being Gallie's right-hand man when it comes to policing. He has the look of a someone you shouldn't upset. The balance is to keep the peace in our displaced little community without going full-on *Animal Farm*. The food continues to arrive, but my ongoing nightmare is that it stops. I convince myself that if Asmus were a cold-blooded killer then I'd already be dead— so would we all. But then the guards ...

Gallie and I take off regularly, sometimes to test each other's sense of reason and strategize. This is generally a failed effort. Sometimes it's because an exchanged glance ignites something. This is always successful.

It's a week, I think, since I was in the mansion. Hugh Wagner tells me I have a visitor, nodding toward the back door of the barn. I'm guessing it's the same visitor I had last time and I take Gallie with me.

There's still a faint shadow of Bess's bruise. She's wrapped in a heavy woolen shawl, shivering in the cool morning air. "Hello Joad," she says, breathing out vapor. She nods at Gallie. She sees I'm looking at the sack she's holding close to her chest so she hands it to me. I open it to see a semi-automatic handgun, and I tilt the bag toward Gallie so she can see it, too. "Kasper gave it to me in a moment of affection. For self defense."

"Did he give you that bruise?" I ask. She looks at Gallie but doesn't answer.

"I need to escape," she says.

"What do you think we can do with this?" Gallie asks, pointing at the sack. Bess looks around cautiously.

"I can get you in the house," she says. Gallie and I exchange a glance. "Middle of the night is best."

"What about the sentries?" Gallie asks.

"They're incompetent. Clowns. For all Kasper's determination and planning, he's never gotten any discipline into them." She shivers. "There's a way in."

"And once we're in?" I ask.

"If you can get your hands on accelerators, that's all you need, right?"

"Maybe," I say. "But I saw the woman in the headset and I'm guessing there's no way we could figure out how to work the technology. It's too different."

"There may be wrist accelerators in there—*our* wrist accelerators," Gallie says.

"But they were programmed to return after four hours."

"Wouldn't Asmus have deprogrammed them?"

"You'd think so. Allowing unattached accelerators to show up at TMA would be asking for trouble. But then, that's how a *rational* lunatic would think."

"And even if they're in there, could we find them? And get to them?" Gallie says.

"I know one thing," Bess says. "Outside of what he calls 'The Center', the house is strictly contemporary, give or take a few weapons. That's how Kasper wants it. We get a lot of high-ranking visitors–British army, mainly."

"Is the Center the place where the arms are received?" I ask. Bess nods. "But that has some kind of biometric scanner for entry doesn't it? How do we get in? Do *you* have access?"

"No, but Mancini does." We ponder this.

"So," I say "if we can get into the house undetected, if we can coerce Mancini into giving access to the Center, if the accelerators are there, if we can find them, and if we can operate them, then this will work."

"Sounds like a plan," Gallie says.

"And I come with you," Bess says as a statement, not a question.

"You come with us," Gallie says. Bess looks at me. I nod. "And once we're back, we figure out how to free the rest. So–"

"Gallie," Bess interrupts. "Can I have a minute with Joad?" Gallie gives me a look that's gone too quickly to interpret, takes the sack from me and disappears into the barn. I'm left with Bess. What now? "Joad, how long were we married in your ... version of things?" She has jumped straight into it.

"Ten years." She smiles and takes a few moments, seeming to prepare whatever she's about to say. "Was I a good wife?" I hesitate too long.

"Yes," I say. "A good wife. Of course you were." She ponders my face and I try to hold an expression consistent with my answer.

"Maybe I shouldn't have been scared off by your father," she says. I work harder on my expression. "Maybe that was just the first in a string of terrible decisions I've made." I smile but neither of us speaks for a moment. "Will you tell me the full story after this is over? Tell me what I missed out on?"

"In appalling detail, unexpurgated" I reply, smiling.

THIRTY-EIGHT

The plan had been made. Admittedly, a plan that calls for more than one miracle is a flawed plan, but it had been the best one Gallie, Bess, Jenn and I could come up with.

It's three AM. Gallie and I are behind the tree line, kneeling and looking at Jenn over the foliage for the signal to go. Our faces are blackened with dirt. My pulse is racing. I'm staying positive despite every impulse of my nature. Unlikely things happen all the time, so why not the success of this plan? Either way, we won't be returning to the barn. I know that much. No possible outcomes have us returning.

Jenn raises her thumb. This is it. That means she saw the flapping curtain. Gallie and I run to the edge of the forest and now we're looking at the back of the mansion. We see the silhouettes of the sentries under the oil lamps at each side of the house, but no one at the back. We exchange a glance that says, *we're really going to do this*, and then we launch ourselves. We're crouched and running toward the mansion. We know that we need to hit our spot the first time. Fumbling around on the grounds will get us caught for sure. Gallie sees it first and pulls my arm. I scan around us as Gallie grabs the hatch handle. If Bess hasn't unbolted it, this is over. Gallie opens the hatch and I exhale. She lowers herself in, I follow and then close the hatch behind me. We pick up the two lit candles waiting for us in their holders. We protect the flames with our palms as we descend the steps and set out along the passageway ahead. It's dank and the light from the candles is feeble, barely illuminating six feet ahead. Gallie looks back at me, her face haunted in its own flickering shadows. I feel for the pistol in my pocket and nod that I'm fine. The passageway is frigid and the air is stagnant. All I can hear is my own panting.

I see a small spot of light ahead. We get closer. It's a keyhole. The passageway ends at the door. I knock. Nothing. This is taking too long. I lift my hand about to knock again and the door opens. Bess is looking back at us.

"He's in the kitchen?" Gallie asks.

"Yes, usual routine. And Kasper's out cold," Bess replies. "Stay behind me." She leads the way. We follow her up the steps from what must be the cellar, she slowly opens the door at the top and puts her head out. No sentries in the house unless there were questionable guests was the rule as Bess had described it. She waves us to follow and we enter what looks like a library, although the tiers of bookshelves that reach to the high ceiling are all empty. We scurry across the room and when she opens the next door, we see the grand staircase. Under it, directly opposite, is the doorway leading to Asmus's Center. I look at Gallie and nod encouragement. Bess tells us to stay put and then runs over to the door. She opens it, looks around, and then beckons us energetically. Once we're all in, she shuts the door and now it's safe to hyperventilate.

"Fuck," I say, and Gallie and Bess agree.

"Now we wait," Bess says. "He usually stuffs his face for about twenty minutes. So it could be any minute now."

"We know what to do?" Gallie asks. We nod. Bess moves down the corridor, I take the middle position and Gallie stands by the door. I remove the handgun from my pocket and we wait. The sound of three people panting fills the long, narrow corridor.

It's an eternity. I look at Bess as if to ask *has something gone wrong?* Then I hear the footsteps. I raise the gun and point it at the door—what I guess to be chest level. Gallie is up against the wall, next to the handle side of the door which we know opens toward the outside. It opens and she reaches out, grabs Mancini by the collar and drags him in. I step forward, rack the pistol slide and point it at his head as Gallie shuts the door behind him.

"Not a word," I hiss. Gallie gives him a shove and I pull him ahead of me. Bess stands aside and I push him forward.

"Seers, hud?" he says, regaining his composure.

"Don't know what the fuck that means, but keep walking."

"It means 'you can't be serious'," he says. "What are you trying to do?" Within a few paces of the door he stops. I push him but he resists. "There's no way I can let you in there. That can't happen."

"Then your 'seers hud' ass will be shot."

"You're not going to shoot me. You're not a murderer. And if you did, where does that get you?"

I'm thinking of my reply when Bess snatches the pistol from me and shoots Mancini. I think it was through the shoulder. He screams and slides down the wall to the ground.

"You shot me," he says in disbelief and nods his head in pain, mouth open. The wall is splattered with blood and he places his hand on his shoulder as the red gushes between his fingers.

"Now this has to go fast," Gallie says. "Real fast." Bess places the gun barrel between Mancini's eyes.

"Okay," he says and I help him struggle to his feet. He faces the door and I hear the clunk of the lock. I push him in, and Gallie and Bess follow. No one is in the room—Bess had been right: Mancini is the entire night shift.

"Accelerators," I yell at him. "Where?" He looks at me but seems more focused on coping with the pain. I tilt my head toward Bess. "Listen to me you little prick. Those accelerators are the only thing between your brains and that artwork. For art's sake, get them."

"I hear yelling," Gallie says, looking out of the door.

"No one's saving you, Mancini," Bess says. "You'll be my final pleasure." He takes what looks like a painful breath then staggers over to a black, smooth wall unit about six feet high. He runs the palm of his good hand across it and a drawer opens smoothly.

"Any second now," Gallie shouts. "No time." I lope to the drawer and see the accelerators inside—our accelerators.

"Gallie, over here," I shout taking out three accelerators and throwing them onto a highly polished baroque tabletop. "Program them. Bess, give me the gun." I take it and stand by the door. Then the door at the far end of the corridor slams open and I fire a burst of shots at it. A guard falls backwards and his rifle clatters on the ground. I hear shouting but no one follows him. I look back at Gallie.

"Just a few seconds," she says, jabbing at an accelerator. The shouting continues as if they're mustering the courage for a full assault. I hear Gallie say to Bess "Hold this. No need to wear it. Then press this. Go!" Then I hear Asmus's voice.

"Get in there you pathetic bastards," I hear him shouting. "They've got one gun between them." He can't know that but he has nothing to lose except a few goons.

"Hey, Kasper," I shout.

"Get in there," he screams.

"Here," Gallie says from behind me. "It's ready, give me the gun."

"No. Leave mine there," I say. "You go." I look back at her and she shakes her head. "Go!" I shout. A hail of fire comes through the door, ripping into furniture, equipment and artwork, and hitting Mancini's crumpled body with enough force to propel him into the far wall. Gallie vanishes. I put my hand around the door and fire off a few shots which are feeble against the incoming bursts but enough to pause them. As I look back to locate my accelerator I hear Asmus screaming at his thugs. I run back and grab the accelerator, holding the wristband tight in my fist. The screen is blank. *Oh, fuck.* I hear the clatter of a multitude of feet coming up the corridor. This is it Joad. The way I die is in a hurricane of lead and steel. I think to touch the screen and it comes to life. But it's got to be too late. I don't look up and I press 'Activate' to the roar of a hundred detonations.

THIRTY-NINE

The ambient light is dimmer and deafening noise is replaced by silence as I fall to the ground. I'm at Gallie's feet and she's looking down at me. Two men are running toward us.

"You okay?" Gallie asks. I pat myself down for pain, blood or holes and then I nod. One of the two men is Boris Zhivov and it takes a second for me to realize I'm lying on the concrete pad of the TMA accelerator facility.

"What the hell happened?" Zhivov asks. "You're caked in crap." I run a finger over my mud-blackened face and inspect it. "And that sounded like a ricochet." I realize a bullet must have gotten into the tachyon blast and finished its journey a couple of centuries after it set out. I check myself again for holes. Gallie pulls me to my feet. I notice the air smells different: cleaner, crisper, metallic.

"Where's–?" I begin and then Bess appears between us and the accelerator cylinder. She arrives standing but then falls backwards with a cry. Gallie and I run over and help her up. Zhivov peers at her.

"One of your team?" he asks.

"No. This is Bess ... Asmus," I reply. Zhivov looks bemused. "She used to be my wife, depending on who you ask," I say. "How long have we been gone?"

142

"An hour maybe," Zhivov replies. So of *course* there was no rescue mission. Temporal logic makes fools of us. "Where are Morales and Byrne?" Gallie and I exchange a glance and she shakes her head. No one is in the mood to explain and Zhivov doesn't press it. We catch our breath in silence. "Nothing personal but why don't you start by taking a shower?"

"Do you have clothes?" Bess asks. "I just want to wear regular clothes."

"I'm afraid you'll all be guests at The Tacky Hotel until we figure out what's happening," Zhivov says. "And don't worry, I'll feed your fucking cat," he tells Gallie pre-emptively. "Toad, your old room is waiting for you." That would have horrified me just a few week ago, but today I'm excited to sink into the plush luxury of its army cot and feel the hot, foul coffee on the back of my throat. "Gallie, you know the routine. Full written report. Take your time and give it to me by two. Got a feeling it might be one of the more interesting ones."

The shower washes away the filth but not the exhaustion. Gallie and I convene in her room to write the report. But first things first. I tell her we don't need separate rooms. After our adventures in every dark corner of the barn loft and every glade of an eighteenth century forest, it's too late to be coy. But like a girlfriend reluctant to get up to anything under her parents' roof, she tells me *no*. I ask for a reminder of whether this is 1996 or 1956. She suggests we get on with the report. I'm going to be just next door, I remind her as I drain my third cup of coffee and she opens the report template with an air of *I'll pretend you didn't say that*.

Zhivov pops his head around the corner to tell us we're meeting with Prasad first thing tomorrow morning and he wants to have fully digested the report before then. *So get the hell on with it*, he leaves unsaid.

How do we resolve this? What does a resolution even

look like? My team needs to be rescued, intact, for sure. But the arms trafficking? How to deal with that? Maybe cut it off at the pass? Prevent it from happening in the first place? No. Prasad had said that following the timeline is always the way to go—the way that doesn't pile on the harm. Mitigate what was done, but don't try to prevent it. But my mind is in no state to try and comprehend that distinction. I got the sense that even the great Prasad himself doesn't have all of this crystal clear in his mind. Gallie types, asks questions, then types more as I look over her shoulder.

FORTY

I'm exhausted but can tell there's no sleep to be had. The red figures on the bedside clock count the passing minutes and it's gone midnight. Truth is, I've gotten used to Gallie's warmth and the sound of her breathing. I hear the rumble of distant thunder and try taking a few deep breaths to settle me.

Then I hear the creak of a door. A silhouette appears briefly against the subdued light of the corridor before the door closes again. I look up through the roof to the heavens. He *does* exist. She sits on the side of my bed and I reach out to touch her leg.

"Hi Joad," Bess whispers.

"What? No. What?" I pull myself up and bring up my knees.

"Did I wake you?" she asks.

"No. Yes. What's wrong?"

"I'm sorry. I startled you."

"No, it's fine. Sorry. I'm exhausted."

"It's just that ... we don't get much chance to be alone. And I think we need to talk, don't we?"

"Do we? Yes. Tomorrow maybe?" I say. "I'm so tired right now. You must be, too."

There's a silence and then she says, "This is weird for me. I know we're closer to home than we just were but that makes it weirder. Do you know what I mean? It's the same and different."

"Yeah, I think so."

"I don't really know what's out there, except that right now there's a ten year-old Elizabeth Sato in Honolulu with her family. How strange is that?" I nod in the dark and there's another silence. "Joad," she says. "I don't want to seem pushy but I've been thinking about something and I just need to say it." *No, no*, I think. "Is that okay?"

"Tomorrow will be better, Bess. I'm barely conscious."

"Should we give it another go? I mean, try to pick it up where we left off?"

"One date is where we left off, Bess." My heart is thudding and I reminisce fondly about the relative comfort of being caught in a spray of automatic gunfire.

"But not in your version, Joad. We were married for a long time. You and me. That's what we can pick up again, can't we?" More silence. "I'm sorry. I'm scaring you." There's a clap of thunder that seems close.

"Bess, the truth is, it wasn't working out that well for us."

"Why not?"

"Well. You know, we're both good people, but we just didn't fit together well. We were going in our own directions. The Bess I knew would agree with that."

"Would she? That's why I'm talking about a fresh start. Literally. How many couples get a chance like this?" She places her hand on my arm. I say nothing. I hear her sigh. "What's wrong with me Joad?"

"Nothing, Bess. Really"

"I'm a disaster. Every decision I make about men is a disaster. I blow you off after a single date and then the men I do pick are bastards and deranged. My last husband wanted to use nuclear weapons against ancient Mongols, and he wasn't even the craziest one. I just want to catch a plane to Honolulu and tell that ten year-old not to turn into such a stupid bitch."

"It's not that—" I start to say, but then I hear the creak of my door and again a silhouette moves across the opening. I fumble to turn on my bedside lamp and squint.

"I'm sorry," Gallie says, pulling her dressing gown tight around herself. "I didn't know you were busy."

"No, I'm not," I say and Bess gives me a discomfited look. "We were just talking about—" I shake Bess's hand off my arm and only then notice that she's wearing nothing but an oversized tee-shirt.

"No, *I'm* sorry. I don't want to interrupt," Gallie says smiling at Bess. With that she leaves.

"Fuck," I say.

"You have more traffic than I-5," Bess says. "What do you think *she* wanted?" I know exactly what she wanted, but not nearly as much as I did.

"Tomorrow Bess. I'm exhausted," I say, lying back down and turning over with finality.

"Okay," she whispers. "Maybe we both have a few things to think about."

FORTY-ONE

In the detection facility meeting room with me is Gallie, Prasad, Zhivov and Abioye. I can't catch Gallie's eye. There's a definite *froideur*. Prasad and Abioye are talking to each other about something that has no meaning to me. Boris is watching Gallie ignore me. It feels like I finally fell asleep last night just as my bedside alarm clock was gearing up to go off. It takes me a moment to notice that Prasad and Abioye have finished their discussion and are now both looking at me. Prasad throws a paper-clipped wad of sheets onto the table that I assume is our report. "Not quite the mission we'd planned on, eh?" he says.

"No," I say. "Although in fairness, I'm not sure we had much of a plan at all." Gallie is finally looking at me, but only to say *yes, embarrassing Prasad and Abioye is the best way to go*. I don't really care about that at this point, although trying to embarrass the great Prasad in this room would be like trying to embarrass someone in front of his dog.

"So his armory is in the mansion?" Prasad asks.

"Pretty sure. Nothing to indicate it's elsewhere," Gallie says.

"Yeah," I agree. "They were offloading crates from his accelerator and loading them onto an elevator that went straight down. We never saw anything being taken away from the mansion." Prasad nods.

"So," he says, addressing Abioye, "dealing with Asmus and his arsenal, and getting the TMA staff home are the two principal objectives."

"Can we send in a force?" Abioye asks in her near-whisper.

"His detection precision is impressive. They must have had our arrival venue pinpointed," I say. "Our security detail didn't stand a chance. To have that level of accuracy based just on the tachyon bow wave is phenomenal."

"It *is* mid-21st technology," Prasad says. "Maybe not too surprising. Is it possible to posture our team for a reduced reaction time?"

"It was almost instantaneous. I heard the gunfire the instant the ambient light changed," Gallie says.

"We could have our security initiate fire as they accelerate," Zhivov says.

"Arrive with guns ablaze?" Abioye says. "A little irresponsible don't you think, Boris?"

"Just a little," Prasad agrees.

"They'd have to be shooting up your accelerator cylinder on this end," I add. There's a silence.

"And Mrs. Asmus is a complication," Prasad says, turning to me. I look at Gallie whose face is stony. "We were not expecting you to bring back a guest."

"She's the reason we could escape," I say.

"We understand that," Abioye says, "but she needs to go back to her place on the timeline." I look around the table.

"What does that mean?"

"How long have you been with TMA?" Zhivov asks. "You know she needs to be sent back."

"To where?"

"Wherever Asmus plucked her from."

"Just how much more do you think the timeline could

be screwed up if she wasn't sent back?" I ask.

"You know better than that Dr. Bevan," whispers Abioye. "We need to minimize the damage." I'm preparing to answer this stupid point when I turn to Gallie and see an almost imperceptible shake of the head. I lean back in my chair. Seconds pass with the clicks of the old electronic wall clock. A question comes to me.

"Where do you focus the detection field for your array?"

"What do you mean?" Zhivov asks. "It's global."

"At ground altitudes?"

"Yes."

"Yeah, same where I'm from."

"So?" Zhivov says.

"Well, that's always made sense," I say. "There's not likely to be much acceleration going on at 30,000 feet. Best detection efficiency if you focus the array on where accelerations are likely to be happening, right?" I seem to be the center of attention, and for the first time it's not in a bad way. "Do you think Asmus follows the same logic?"

FORTY-TWO

Gallie and I are by the barn, or at least where the barn had once stood. There are no remains of it although the ground has somehow retained a faint memory through the subtle shading of the pristine grass. The cloudless midday sky is an unrealistic shade of dark blue. We stand where we had stood over two centuries earlier. The forest is no longer there, although we can see trees in the distance, and has been replaced by well-kempt meadows. Prasad is talking to a man in military fatigues who had been here when we arrived. Behind them is a grand building that is, according to the ornate signage over the archway leading to its grounds, *The Leatown Retreat and Spa*. The building looks larger than the mansion that once stood there, and in the front grounds there are cafe tables under umbrellas where guests are being served by white-coated waiters. On a gazebo, a brass quartet is playing show tunes and a small audience is gathered around them.

"My, Leatown has moved on," I say. We had walked down earlier to where Leatown once stood; where we had narrowly escaped a beating or worse. There was no metropolis in its place, and not even the ruins of a colonial town. It seems Leatown had not been destined to be the seed of a great American city. Any residue of it now lies beneath the 5th and 6th holes of a golf course, and the town's only monument is a spa for the wealthy.

It was within a few hours of our debrief that we found ourselves back in Leatown. "The air's different, isn't it?" I say. "It just smells and feels different."

"No unwashed TMAers to stink it up," Gallie replies.

"Not that. Do you think each age has its own air? Two hundred and some years of history has to leave its mark, doesn't it? Industries, technologies, wars, just generations of life. It can't leave the air unchanged." Gallie doesn't reply. Maybe she has no opinion on the matter, or maybe she won't break a streak of not looking at me today. Zhivov returns from his circuit of the building and stops to talk to the woman who had accompanied him. They shake hands and she walks off toward the vehicles parked on the road that runs parallel to the once-was wagon path. Zhivov strides toward Prasad and we follow him.

Gallie and I are introduced to a Colonel Ahmed, who seems to be a relaxed and amiable fellow with none of the hard edges you might expect of a soldier. He smiles and comments on the unseasonably warm weather.

"Our local historian confirms this place is built on the same site as the old chateau," Zhivov says. "It's about twice the footprint of the original structure but the east boundaries of the old and new structures coincide."

"How far is the east wall from the barn site?" Prasad asks.

"About a hundred yards," Gallie answers.

"That a problem?" Prasad asks the colonel.

"No, shouldn't be," he answers. We watch the activity in the front grounds of the Leatown Retreat and Spa.

"Is croquet your game?" I ask Prasad.

"Cricket," he replies. Of course. I look back toward where the barn had been. Our barn. Temporal logic is such a quagmire. I think of my friends (because that's what they are) still suffering. Yet that suffering happened over two centuries ago. But that's a bullshit theoretical detail. They're suffering until we put a stop to it. Yet, in some way, we either did or didn't put a stop to it–we succeeded or we didn't and it's a settled matter. And still, that's not true; it's not set in stone. A park just appeared in Risley in place of the shopping mall that thought it was set in stone. It just wasn't. If anything about temporal logic was seeming to get more comprehensible to me after all of this, then it was slipping away from me again.

I'd asked Gallie to walk with me as Prasad, Zhivov and the colonel plan their plans. We're on the edge of where the woods had begun. I'm thinking of what we did in those woods. Is she thinking about that too?

"You know, Bess just came in, uninvited," I say. "At first I thought it was you. I was a happy man."

"And just how far did you get before you realized it wasn't me?"

"She terrified me at 'hello'," I say. Gallie stares at me for a moment then breaks into a smile.

"I know," she says. "I saw her walk past my door. I was coming in to rescue you." I'm aghast.

"Why did you leave it so long?" I ask. "I was in serious trouble."

"I didn't want to get between a man and his other-worldly wife."

"You bitch," I say. "You were testing me."

"I wasn't, so get over it. Besides, you passed."

"If there was a barn or a tree anywhere near, I'd take you behind it."

"Would you? Maybe I'd let you."

FORTY-THREE

I join Gallie in her room to nuke a late supper and drink cheap white wine. I propose a toast. "To our 2021 colleagues, assholes to a person, but soon to be freed assholes." *Freed assholes* Gallie echoes.

"You know, I'm not sure I could work in your TMA," Gallie says putting down her glass.

"I know. Everyone is so damn collegial here," I say. "It was the first thing I noticed. Where did we go wrong?"

"Well, luckily, your nasty work environment didn't have any serious consequences. Oh ... Kasper Asmus." I take the nuked food out of the microwave and inspect it with disgust. A dessert compartment of red goo has bubbled over into an orange-colored compartment of first course matter.

"Is it going to work?" I ask. Gallie's smile fades.

"I think so, Joad."

"So many people could be hurt. Here *and* there."

"We'll take every–"

"And it is a demented plan, isn't it? I mean, barking."

"It's not like we had to pick between this one and a sensible plan. We're taking the path of least crazy. It'll work."

"Okay, " I say, but it's not okay. It's several tachyon blasts away from okay. We scrape up our dinners and eat. Then we pour more wine and lie back on the cot, Gallie's head on my chest. I curl her chestnut hair around my finger. "Abioye is pretty strict on the rules," I say.

"She's TMA through and through," Gallie replies.

"So Bess has to go back to 2030 or wherever. No ifs, ands, or buts."

"No ifs, ands, or buts." Gallie looks up at me. "It's why we exist. What we're all about."

"I know," I say. "And what about me?" Gallie looks away. "I have to go back to 2021 after all this is over, no ifs ands or buts?" She doesn't answer. "I'm not happy with that. I'm where I want to be right now." Gallie remains silent. "There's nothing I want in 2021. All that's there for me is a crappy, dilapidated house and a job I don't want any more. And not ... this." Gallie kisses me. "We can disappear can't we? Disappear somewhere in time." Gallie smiles.

"Floating through time and space forever, star-crossed lovers," she whispers into my chest.

"We can do that."

"What a nightmare for TMA. Two of their team spitting on every principle they stand for, causing havoc across eternity. Home-grown vandals."

"You're overplanning, Gallie. We just need to vanish. Never be heard from again." I know I'm not supposed to see it, but Gallie wipes a tear from her eye before she sits up.

"You know we can't do that," she whispers and refills her glass. "I hate it but the universe just didn't line us up. You're out there, but you're ten years old. That's the one second per second Joad the universe gave me."

"The universe? The universe is a dumbass. If it wasn't, there'd by no job for TMA. You know that, Gallie. We have careers built on correcting the mistakes the universe makes."

Gallie smiles. "But not that kind of mistake, Joad."

"You really don't want to fight this?" I ask.

"Fight it? And then what? Go back to our TMA careers having violated all it stands for?" She strokes my cheek. "Yes I want to fight it. I want to fight it like hell because I love you." She shakes her head. "But then we'd be different people."

The next two weeks are spent planning. This time, I'm inside the tent, but this time, I'm not sure I want to be. Priority 1, the plan has it, is to neutralize Asmus and his arms business. Priority 2 is the rescue mission for the TMA team, provided they haven't been annihilated by Priority 1. It's a plan that TMA can't pull off by itself. The only room secured for videocons with our collaborators is in the accelerator facility, and so each day I have a commute. I get back to the detector facility late in the evenings and Bess, by then aching for company, seeks me out. I do feel sorry for Bess. She, Gallie and I are stuck here, the thought being that we can't rule out Asmus coming after us. After all, if Asmus would try to take me out just because I agreed with the many who thought he was a weird little shit, imagine what he'd want to do to me for kidnapping his wife.

So there's a lot of time to fill with Bess. I tell her about her would-be life in Risley, but avoiding her would-be life with me. Bess enjoys that she was emerging as a world-class winemaker in that other world, because this Bess knows nothing of wine. I tell her about the Dog Star Winery and Vineyard. Den isn't part of my story.

Abioye had asked me to be the one who tells Bess about TMA's plans for us. I do and Bess takes it poorly. "There's nothing for me in 2030. No, I'm not going back there. Not a chance." Maybe I'm not the one to make the argument to her.

"I hear you. Not a hell of a lot for me where I came from, either."

"Then fuck them, Joad. You and me. We go where we

want to," Bess says. I want to be right here is what I'm thinking. "I'm alone there. No, fuck them. I'm not going back there." So that went as well as it deserved to. But her anger inflames mine. These rules that are stealing our lives are rules based on a hard vacuum of comprehension. Someone thinks it's the safest way to go, but no one really understands a damn about temporal logic. So Asmus alters the timeline–the British beat the Americans and so there's no American nation. Who's to say that's better or worse than our version. So we're governed by a fuckwit parliament instead of a fuckwit congress? So the Vikings have their asses handed to them and that's a disaster? What are we trying to preserve? Our own little version? Why? Why should Bess and I be victims of that? There's no logic behind it. There's no logic behind anything. So the British win because of the weapons Asmus supplies, and it's the Second Amendment that helps him get his hands on those weapons, and the Second Amendment is part of the American Constitution. How does any of that work? And this thin comprehension of what's actually going on is behind the stubborn need for me to be flung back to 2021? No one knows how to stir up a rage in Joad Bevan like Joad Bevan does. And Gallie is always the one who soothes the pain for me. But Bess has only me to lean on. She has been dealt a crappy hand.

FORTY-FOUR

We drive in the night between TMA facilities. I'm with Zhivov and in the car ahead is Prasad, Abioye and Gallie. I'm as cold as ice and shivering. We may be about to kill people—a lot of innocent people—if something goes wrong. We drilled this three times over the week. The confidence I felt after the last drill has now drained from me. What's about to happen is the real thing. *It'll be alright on the night* is an expression I've heard over the years, yet in my experience *the night* can innovate screw-ups that the rehearsals just didn't have the imagination to think of.

The first drill was a disaster. The accelerator aircraft completely missed its target, accelerating nothing but fresh air, and a missile buried itself at Mach 3 into wasteland ten miles north of the TMA site. That shook us all up and the plan was nearly dropped on the spot. The missile we're about to launch tonight, the one with a high explosives warhead, won't be hitting wasteland if it all goes pear-shaped. I open my window to get a breath of night air.

The second drill had gone to plan, as far as we could tell. The fighter launched its missile, the accelerator aircraft fired its beam and hit its target, and the missile popped like a bubble. If our programming was right, a few protomammals likely got a shock. The third drill went about the same. But these drills couldn't validate the full parameter set. Did the missile retain orientation? Did the homing system successfully reset? There's too much that needs to happen on the far side of the accel–too much we didn't test–to be confident.

This is the room we've sat in for the past week–drilling, analyzing, anguishing, arguing, reanalyzing. Tonight there's silence but for the hum of the air conditioner. We wait. We keep waiting. The analog wall clock reaches eleven PM and the large monitor at the foot of the table comes to life to display the US Air Force crest. We're streaming the Kellerman AF Base.

"Good evening. Kellerman here." It's the voice of Colonel Ahmed.

"Roger that," Zhivov replies.

"We're counting down 5 minutes and 20 seconds. Stand by."

We look at each other. No words are spoken. Abioye, who is usually the epitome of calm and cold reason, is biting her fingernails. We may find out what her talk-out-loud voice sounds like before the night is over. I begin to rock in my chair and immediately get a disapproving look from Gallie. Is it too late to come up with a better plan? One slightly less insane than the guy we're trying to neutralize? Yes, it is too late. It's much too late. I rock again. Gallie will just have to deal with it. Nothing is in our hands at this point. We decided on it, we planned it, we brought together the team to deploy it, and now what the plan requires is that we sit dumbly and wish that we'd kept in touch with a god to pray to. The Air Force crest has vanished and now the screen is dark and grainy but for yellow digits in the top left corner counting down from 4 minutes and 12 seconds. I hear indistinct voices in the background and over them Ahmed announces "Four minutes." Right here we seem to be breaking the *one second per second* rule in that this seems eternal. Prasad stands and leans against the wall. I see Gallie is now rocking in her chair and I shake my head at her. She smiles.

In the grainy image an object becomes discernible and a crosshairs appears on it. "Target fixed," Ahmed says. The object is the outline of the Leatown Resort and Spa. If only those poor bastards knew.

"The evacuation happened?" I ask.

"Of course it did." Zhivov replies. "As far as we know. Just relax Toad." This means that the resort occupants had been bussed away *en masse* ("as far as we know") in response to a fake bomb threat, although *fake* is not exactly the right word here. I stand up and pace.

"Accel flight positioned," I hear Ahmed say. Then I hear a second voice.

"Confirm, Kellerman," she says. I know her voice from the drills, but not her name. She's the commander of the second aircraft–the one carrying the accelerator. Hell, this can't work. What were we thinking? "Euler orientation for accel is set and confirmed." Okay, this ensures the missile has the same orientation after it's acceled and comes out the other side–if it works.

"Four, three, two, ..." Ahmed counts down "... one, launch." I hear a faint voice saying *launch confirmed*. A set of numbers appears at the bottom on the monitor. The first figure is the elevation of the missile. That's the one that has all my attention. If that number hits zero, then a resort and spa becomes a crater. "Eleven seconds to accel ... ten, nine ... standing by to switch homing signal ... seven, ..." Okay, so at the moment of acceleration, the homing system needs to deactivate and then reactivate, and then the destination becomes an eighteenth century mansion instead of a twentieth century spa. In theory, just fine, provided the missile comes out at the correct orientation. " ... five, four three, ..."

"Targeted." It's the woman's voice. I'm tracking: 17,000

feet, 16,000 feet. "Beam on," she says. I'm not breathing. 15,000 feet, 14,000 feet. Jesus. Way too low. "That's a miss," she says calmly.

"Fuck," Zhivov says just before me. Abioye jumps to her feet.

"Instruct to abort?" Ahmed asks. At least it sounds like a question.

"Negative, retargeting." 12,000 feet, 11,000 feet. My hands are on my head and my heart is hammering hard on my rib cage. 10,000 feet. "That's a hit." The elevation counter freezes at 10,000 feet.

"Agghh," I shout, but it's drowned by cheers. Gallie grabs me for a tight hug. Prasad's fists are raised in victory and Abioye's hands part so we can see her face again.

"That was some bullshit," Zhivov says.

"Bullshit indeed," says Prasad. Then Gallie shushes us as the female voice begins to report out.

"Orientation, spatial and temporal coordinates all within tolerance," she says with a casual professionalism. "Sorry about the hiccup." This woman must have liquid nitrogen in her arteries. In my mind's eye I see the fireball that devours the mansion and its arsenal. I see Asmus evaporate at its white hot core. I see the barn untouched and its occupants enjoying the fireworks. I see a smoldering crater. It would be more than nice if what I'm seeing anything approaches what actually happened.

FORTY-FIVE

There's a certain *joie de vivre* among us that's probably unjustified, but I'll take it. The strike was timed for one week (local time) after the day Gallie, Bess and I escaped. The thinking was that that was enough margin to ensure a slight temporal miss wouldn't put us in the target zone. The temporal logic of that thinking is a quagmire but I couldn't have begun to come up with a counterargument. Then, the rescue mission is timed for three days after the strike. Again, that gives some margin, but not too much because the TMAers are not the survivalist types. Of course, three days on the far end translates to as much time as we need at our end. We just need to program the accelerators to land at the right time and place.

In the euphoric aftermath of the strike, Abioye and Prasad relax the lockdown. They're not dumb enough to think that Asmus or his goons wouldn't have plenty of time between our escape and the strike to come after us. But they're not immune to the *zeitgeist* of the moment and must have figured they'd take a few risks.

I could have visited the Bevans again–my home, my father's bar, myself. The thought of introducing Bess to my dad was an amusing one. A weakness of mine has always been that I'm prone to act on amusing thoughts. Profound thoughts, compassionate thoughts, pragmatic thoughts, spiritual thoughts, creative thoughts, erotic thoughts are all fine, but any imbecile can have those. Amusing thoughts are the ones I respect. But this amusing thought is just too hazardous. After all, Bess is the woman who put a bullet into someone out of sheer impatience. I don't think much of my father but I don't want to find out what Bess might do to a man who she thinks prevented a blissful married life.

The first couple of outings had been no more than car rides around town—Bess, Gallie and myself—with Gerard Bruce, the head of security, as chauffeur. Bruce carried a hand gun, and I had seen him put a much larger, nastier weapon into the car trunk. The excitement of getting off the TMA site, even for nothing more than a ride, had been exhilarating. But now, the third outing is the one Bess had been lobbying for. It's a trip to the vineyards.

Bess has a yearning to learn about her once and never-was career as a talented winemaker. It's both funny and sad. Funny that you'd want to reminisce about something that never happened to you. Sad because for all the marital misery, it would have been a better life than the one she actually had.

We drive up the slope of Red Mountain, and where in my day there will be twenty wineries, today there are only a couple. I point out to Bess where her Dog Star Winery will one day stand. Her smile is silly and beguiling. There are no vines there yet, just undeveloped land. I think of the times I'd been late to arrive there, to Bess's savage irritation. But that's just a dream now.

The winery we pick is in the style of a rustic Tuscan villa. We sit at the tasting room bar and sample the winery's offerings, making appreciative and engaged sounds as the server talks about terroir and a winemaker who gave up a career in accounting for all of this. Through large plate glass

windows we see acres of vines under the encroaching
shadow of the mountain top as the sun begins to set. I look
behind us to see Bruce sitting at his own table, on which sits
a plastic bottle of water. He's surveying the other guests
with comic suspicion.

Bess wangles an introduction to the winemaker and is
deep in conversation with him. If I know Bess, and if this
Bess is like the one I know, then she's contemplating a
revival of the career she never had. But maybe it's less
innocent than that. He seems to be under her spell. It's
weirdly like home. I had never enjoyed wine stuff—the
endless releases, events, parties—yet being here has a
comforting familiarity. I always found the wine industry to
be its own cure because, ultimately, it's about nice booze.

Gallie and I are left to ourselves. Having downed a
couple of indistinguishable yet apparently very different
Cabernets gives me courage to take another run at the
reasons I should stay. It doesn't take long to realize that this
was a mistake, and so I shut up and just hold Gallie's hand.
We speak nothing of matters TMA, of the strike or of the
rescue plans. Instead, I learn about Gallie's cat and Boris's
kindness in fostering it. It's a topic so ridiculous for the
Gallie I've come to know that I hang on every word. It
seems that a man I had first taken as something of a little
prick is really quite an Assisi. I admit that Boris has grown
on me. I've never mentioned to anyone the high mantle that
he was to assume, but wondered how many TMAers I might
have come to respect if I'd gotten past my first impressions.
Yet changing the timeline is one thing, but changing Joad
Bevan, now there's a serious challenge.

Gallie and Bess join forces to visit the bathroom. I see a
risk there. Even stone cold sober, Bess would be a worry.
But Gallie can handle anything, I think. I look around the
bar which is now filling up. A guy a few seats up from me
looks familiar. Not a TMAer, for sure. I suppose I was
bound to see someone the young Joad had known. A
teacher maybe? I'm at an age where teachers look like kids

so it's possible. An older kid from school? No, too old for that. I down another glug of wine and look at the shadows growing over Red Mountain. I turn back to the guy at the bar who is now looking at me. I smile and nod. Maybe he's going to solve the mystery for me. He smiles back widely. My heart misses a beat. *Oh Fuck!* I leap from my seat sending it flying backwards and lope toward the women's restroom. I notice Bruce has gone. I burst through the door and Gallie and Bess look up, startled from their conversation. A woman exiting a stall looks at me in horror before reversing back in.

"We gotta go, now." I shout. "They're here." They ask no questions and follow me out. I see the kitchen entrance and run through the swinging doors. Kitchens always have back doors, don't they? It's where the chef goes to smoke. We run, navigating steel counters and cupboards toward the 'Exit' sign. We emerge in the back parking lot. Twenty yards away there's a knot of men in conversation who don't notice us. Again, I thank god for the incompetence of the slobs Asmus employs. But if we try to get to our car, we'll be seen for sure. Where the hell is Bruce? Asmus's goons are standing between us and where we need to be, although without Bruce and his keys, the car is useless to us. I point to the beginning of the vineyard that borders the parking lot. Crouched, we run into the vines. Then I hear shouting, but the heavy vernacular is impossible to understand.

"What happened to Bruce?" Bess asks. "What good is a guard who vanishes just when a guard is what you need?"

"Can you see anything?" Gallie whispers. "*I* can't."

"I'm not putting my head up," I say. There are enough leaves on the vines to keep us concealed, but also enough to prevent our seeing what's happening. We look down the aisle of vines and it's long without an end in sight.

"We could just keep going," Gallie says. "It must come out somewhere."

"Once they pass this row, they'll see us no matter how far we get." I say. "We'd be like pins in a bowling lane."

"I'll strangle Bruce if I survive this," Bess whispers. "He could be picking them off like sitting ducks. I know these dirtbags."

"The car is a mobile arsenal," I say. "If we could get to it–"

"Without a key?" Gallie whispers.

"You know," Bess says, "I'm put right off winemaking."

Two black, shiny boots land in front me. It happened too fast to be sure, but I think Gallie had balanced on her hands and kicked out hard with the soles of her feet, bringing the owner of the boots down on top of me. As I pull myself from under him, another one of them jumps the vines and I see Bess lunge at him. She's too light to bring him down but as he takes a couple of steps backwards, it gives me a chance to take a run at him, jump and kick him in the stomach. We hit the ground at the same time. I see Gallie, red-faced and struggling fiercely with the first man she had brought down. He's on his ass holding on to her rather than fighting. I try to get up to help but then stars fill my head and I stagger sideways into the vines. I hear a voice asking if I'm okay. It's Bess. Gallie and the man she's struggling with are there, and then they're not. It takes me seconds to realize that they've popped out. Accelerated. Bess is kneeling by me, holding my hand and looking into my face. Then I turn to see the barrel of a gun pointing at me.

"No," I hear someone shout. " 'ee didn't say to kill no one."

"Yer better not," another voice says. Then there's suddenly quiet but for the vines rustling in the evening breeze.

"They've gone," Bess says. The stars are dispersing and I feel a trickle on my forehead.

"They wanted Gallie," I whisper.

FORTY-SIX

Bess helps me into the van. Zhivov is driving and Prasad is in the back row.

"How the hell didn't you detect them coming?" is the first thing I say.

"Are you okay?" Zhivov asks.

"There must have been little or no uptime bow wave," says Prasad.

"No, didn't see 'em coming," Zhivov adds.

"How is that possible?" Bess pulls the sliding door closed and we take off with a jog.

"You've got to remember they have technology we don't," Prasad says, with irritating calm.

"Gallie is gone," I say, lightly touching the egg on the back of my skull. "Accelerated. Bruce too, maybe."

"How didn't anyone in there see Bruce vanish?" Bess asks.

"Maybe they did. We were out of there too fast to ask."

"Where do you think they've taken her?" Bess asks. I try to think through the pain.

"Between the escape and the strike," I say. "Must be."

"Make sense," Zhivov says. "He'd come looking for you after you got away, and, hope to god, he'd be in no condition to be doing anything after the strike."

"We'll confirm that," Prasad says.

"So now our plans change," I say.

"No," Prasad replies.

"Yes they do. Now Gallie is probably in the mansion—the one that'll be a crater."

"Or she'll wind up in the barn with the others," Prasad says. I look back at him and wince with the pain it causes.

"You want us to take that risk? This was a tit-for-tat mission. I took his wife and he takes Gallie. Those goons had no orders to kill anyone, or to do anything but abduct Gallie. Asmus wanted her and I'm betting he's going to keep her close."

"I understand," Prasad says, "but you know we can't send anyone in until after the strike. We've been through that and nothing has changed. They'd be dead on arrival, literally. No way around it."

"Nothing has changed?" I echo, incredulously. "A fuck load has changed. Just now, everything changed. We're not going to let Jane Galois get incinerated by a missile that *we fired*." I look at Zhivov but he says nothing, his eyes on the road. Bess is staring at me.

"Missile strike?" she says.

The medic exits after having applied something to my head that stung like hell. The detector facility sick bay is a bed, two chairs, a chunky computer and monitor, a metal sink, a poster describing the benefits of a healthy diet, and a few primitive-looking machines. Bess and Zhivov are silent.

"We're not going to let this happen," I say.

"No, we're not," Zhivov replies. I'm nonplused. I'd said it to begin the argument. Are we talking about different things? Is Zhivov straying from the company line? I know his type. The company line, rational or irrational, fair or unfair, smart or idiotic, is what they defend beyond all reason. You don't get to be the Director of TMA any other way.

"We're going to get Gallie out of there?" I ask, waiting to be corrected.

"Yes, we are."

"You mean talk your boss around?" Bess asks.

"That's not possible," Zhivov says. "There's no talking Prasad out of anything. And his logic isn't wrong."

"You're telling me you're willing to go against Prasad's will?" I ask but don't risk waiting for an answer. "Any ideas? How do we prevent popping up inside a hurricane of bullets?"

"I did have an idea," he says. "It'd been too unhinged to bring up, but like you said, things have changed." I turn toward Bess who gives me the look of a child whose parents had better not be thinking *it's your bedtime.* "How many men does Asmus have?" he asks Bess.

"Ten, a dozen. No more than that. Why?"

"Ever heard of Russian Roulette?"

Zhivov locks the deadbolt on the sick bay door. "A dozen men ready to shoot the crap out of whoever shows up before they can do a thing about it." He smirks. "But say they detect twenty, thirty arrivals, all simultaneous. Arrivals dispersed all around."

"Twelve goons, thirty arrivals."

"Let's make it twelve goons, fifty arrivals."

"And I'm one of the arrivals," I say. "Who are the others?"

"*We're* one of the arrivals," Zhivov says. "The other forty nine are no one. They're accelerators accelerating pure fresh air."

"Russian Roulette," I say. "If Asmus and his goons pick *our* acceleration, that's the bullet in the chamber?"

Zhivov nods. "Is it crazy?"

"Yes, it's crazy," Bess replies for me.

"And you didn't mention your career-ending idea to

Prasad?"

"You'd take that risk," Bess asks me. I nod. "And you?" Zhivov nods.

"You can round up fifty accelerators?"

"I can."

"And weapons?"

"Weapons? Okay Rambo. Now that we've taken the taint off *crazy*, we may as well go for it."

FORTY-SEVEN

I've come to notice there's a pattern to TMA planning. It involves a lot of specifics on how to get to where you need to be, alive, and then from there it plummets on detail. This plan is no exception. In fairness, there's not much to base a plan on. Gallie is either in a mansion or in a barn. The third option, that she's in neither, is outside the bounds of the feeble plan we've stitched together. The plan has it that we arrive, well-armed, three days after we had escaped, and about the same amount of time before the missile strike. As we arrive, so do another fifty tachyons bursts carrying nothing but air. The plan—the prayer—is that our personal tachyon burst is not among the ones that get enveloped in a hail of lead. This is where the strategy plummets and we lean on pure luck. What we do is go in there, find Gallie and bring her home. My private strategy is to also deal with Asmus in a conclusive way. Not figuring into the strategy is that Boris and I lack even a rudimentary training on the weapons we'll be taking with us.

I have a couple of days to spend with Bess as Zhivov goes about his business of collecting the inventory of tools for our wild plan. Because of the stupidity of time, there's no big rush on preparing, but it's not the temporal logic that's driving us. It's that my heart is in my mouth and every second that passes without knowing what's happening to Gallie is agony.

If Bess is still trying to give a second chance to the marriage she never had, she's concealing it well. But she *is* serious about restoring the career she never had. We talk wine to the limits of my knowledge. One thing about which there's no uncertainty is that she has no intention of going home, and no patience for anyone dumb enough to bring it up.

"Prasad can fuck off to 2030 if he likes, but I'm going nowhere."

"Can't think about that right now."

"I know."

The night of the mission has arrived. My room is where it starts, and Bess and I are waiting for Zhivov to show up with his final box of tricks.

"You going to keep each other safe?" Bess asks. She takes my hand and squeezes it.

"Yes. You know, I had Boris all wrong. First impressions weren't good, but thank god for him." I notice my hand is shaking a little so I pull it from Bess's grip. "He's not who I thought he was. Breaking the rules. He's a surprise."

"Really?" Bess says with a faint smile.

"Yeah."

"Why is it the smartest people are sometimes the dumbest people?" Bess says. She's shaking her head. "Didn't you know?"

"What?"

"If your regular IQ was equal to your emotional IQ, you'd never have gotten the gist of breathing," Bess says. "Boris is head-over-heals for Gallie Galois. How can't you see that? I'm guessing he has been for years."

"No."

"Yes. And then *you* fall out of the blue."

"You think they–?"

"No. He has the look of a man who's never dared act on it. I wish I knew how not to act on things. My downfall, I'm afraid." I smile. She doesn't know it but she had said that same thing to me once before, and my mind turns to Den, the wine entrepreneur and stealer of wives. "Maybe that's why Jane Galois has men beating her door down and Elizabeth Sato ... doesn't."

Zhivov bursts in carrying the final box. All furniture had been stacked against the walls to make room for his inventory. Boxes of accelerators, eighteenth century clothes and weapons. First he lays out the wrist accelerators across the floor in neat rows. One at a time he programs them, all fifty. They look of different designs and vintages but they'd better all have the same precision. Them arriving even minutes apart turns the game from Russian roulette to straight-up carnage.

Next we kit up in the breeches, boots, jackets and tricorns. We get an assault rifle each with spare clips and a solid movie-based understanding of how to reload. Zhivov ushers us to the corner of the room to keep out of the tachyon inner blast radii of the unmanned wrist accelerators. We wait, and then like fireworks, the accelerators pop off in twos and threes. They'll be highly curious picking up these accelerations in the detector control room not a hundred yards from here, but they'll have no time to do a damn thing about it. After the last one pops, Zhivov and I stand back to back, guns aimed forward, our eyes along their sights, just like we'd seen people do it who know what the hell they're doing. Zhivov pops off first. I have that feeling you get when you know that in less than a second you could be shredded in a hailstorm of lead and steel. I should be looking along the barrel of my gun, but my last glimpse of 1996 is Bess's face and the incredulity etched into it.

FORTY-EIGHT

The first thing I notice is that I'm not being shredded in a hailstorm of steel and lead. The second thing is a camp of white tents, campfires and the twilit silhouettes of men that extend as far as the eye can see. This is the wrong place. Where the hell am I? I turn to see a group of men clustered around the closest campfire and looking directly at me. I drop my gun and tell Zhivov to do the same thing, although I'm not a hundred percent sure he's still behind me.

"Did you see that?" one of the men says, as they get to their feet. They're holding rifles although they're not in any kind of uniform. Once more, I'm at the wrong end of several gun barrels.

"Don't want any trouble," I say because that's all I can think of, as if I'm dealing with a mugger and not a thousand-strong army. I'm sure that my not wanting any trouble is coming as a great relief to them.

"It's all good," I hear Zhivov say. *They just came out of nothing. What you mean? Just then. You harecop. Magicked from thin air. They did. Get the lieutenant. You get 'im.* As my eyes adapt to the dark I see that we've landed exactly where we had meant to. The mansion is at the center of the vast landscape of tents and the barn is behind us.

"What's happening?" Zhivov asks me.

"This is one hell of any army," I say. The two men who approach us are unmistakably soldiers, probably officers. They're wearing the blue jackets of the Continental Army with yellow breeches and black boots. They look us over and someone hands them one of our weapons.

"They were carrying these?"

"Yes, they're ours," I reply before anyone else has the chance, "but we put them down. We're not your enemies." The officer turns to his colleague.

"These are the swift guns," he says. He looks back at us. "Where are you from?" He called them swift guns. He's seen them before.

"We're from ..." Where are we from? "We're Americans."

"We're patriots," Zhivov says.

"*Are* you?" the officer asks with what seems like a hint of sarcasm, although I wouldn't know how to make that call any more. He whispers something to the other officer. "Come," he says and walks off. The other officer gives me a shove to follow.

The Leatown garrison must have been taken. There couldn't have been forty or fifty British troops there, and even if they had had the 'swift guns', which I'm not sure Asmus would have let happen so close to home, I doubt that they could have fended off an army of this size. I look toward the barn but it's just a shadow against dark. I'm pushed to keep walking.

"Not in the plan," I hear Zhivov say behind me, followed by invective after the shove it earned him.

We're in the entrance hall with the grand staircase in front of us. There must be a dozen soldiers here alone. I notice that the weapons are purely eighteenth century and that these soldiers, unlike Asmus's slobs, are standing still, straight and alert. I scan the space. I could see Gallie at any moment, I tell myself, but then fear bubbles up. How did this army take Leatown? Was it violent, a battle? Was Gallie

175

hurt, or worse? Is she even here? Prasad had confirmed that this is where she'd arrived after being taken. But Asmus is a madman. He could have since flung her a thousand years back to die. Or just killed her on arrival.

We're told to wait and one of the officers enters what I know to be the drawing room. Zhivov and I are facing each other. I realize we're still wearing the wrist accelerators. This could be our escape. If it is, we better decide fast because in that drawing room there may be someone who knows what these things can do. But if we accelerate, then what? We get nowhere. No, we need to see this through. Gallie could be in that room. If she is I could lunge for her and accelerate us both. The programming is already in place and a touch of the 'Activate' key will take us to where we need to be. I notice Zhivov is looking alternately at me and my accelerator. He's having a similar thought. I nod. But it then occurs to me that he may be thinking something different entirely—that we should pop off right now. Then the drawing room door opens and the officer beckons us. I take a deep, slow breath to settle my shaking.

Gallie is there, seated. I exhale. I look at Zhivov who glances back at me before returning his attention to Gallie. A smile flicks across her face. In front of us is a soldier, clearly of high rank. He's wearing a coat of blue with gold epaulettes and trim, and his hand is resting on the grip of his sword. On each side of him but a step back are two other senior-looking officers. I scan the room to see half a dozen soldiers standing to attention, eyes forward. And there's one more figure. It's Kasper Asmus. He's grinning as someone approaches us from behind and rips our accelerators from us.

The general looks us over without expression. "And who are you?" he asks. The accent is unusual and I can't place it. Not American. Not French. Maybe some form of British. We tell him our names. "And where are you from?"

Zhivov and I exchange a glance. What answer will keep us alive? It's time to resort to the truth, I decide.

"Washington state," I reply. The general's expression is unperturbed.

"What did you say about Washington?"

"It's ... it's the place I'm from. Originally. Traveled around a bit. Needed to get away from home for a while. But I landed back in Washington." It wasn't a well thought-out tactic but perhaps babbling will make me seem open, safe and responsive. Or just too unbalanced to press. "A lot of people wind up where they grew up. Maybe it's just lack of imagination but I think a person is attracted back to their roots. I have friends from Ohio who—" The general raises a finger to stop me. I'm grateful. Gallie is looking at me incredulously. I shrug.

"General Penrose, may I?" It's Asmus. I brace myself. The general nods.

"This fellow is a close friend of mine. I'm pleased you found him. I've been quite worried about his welfare. And Mr. Zhivov is also an acquaintance." He grins. "You're looking well Boris. You seem more youthful and healthy than when I last saw you. Good for you, good for you." One of the officers behind the general steps forward to whisper something in his ear. Penrose raises his finger again.

"You were in possession of the swift guns. May I enquire what you intended to do with them?"

"We surrendered them to your troops General," Zhivov says. "They were for our self defense." Penrose calmly assesses this response.

"You may be aware that Mr. Asmus has made some rather outlandish claims about his origin," Penrose says. Asmus begins to pipe up but Penrose raises the *shut up* finger. "You will be quiet Mr. Asmus." Asmus looks like he might be about to protest, but then thinks better of it. "Mr. Bevan, Mr. Zhivov, I'll ask you again. Where are you from?" His calm belies the possibility of him ordering something dire.

Zhivov and I look at each other, and then at Gallie. She gives an almost imperceptible shrug. "It may seem an unlikely story," Zhivov says, "but we'll be truthful with you, sir. My colleague—"

"The future," I say. "Well, your future. That's where we're from. Twenty-first century to be specific. *I* am anyway. We traveled back in time to be here. The guns we were carrying we brought with us."

Penrose raises his eyebrows. It's the first human response I've seen from him. Asmus is grinning. I take this to mean my story is consistent with his.

"If I may General," Asmus says. There's no finger raised to stop him. "It does seem implausible, I know. But could there be a plausible explanation of the swift guns? These weapons incorporate inventions unknown in the here and now, I'm sure you'll agree, sir." Penrose neither agrees nor disagrees.

"And what is your purpose?" Penrose asks. A bloody good question. Asmus grins. Penrose holds out his hand and one of his officers places a semi-automatic pistol in it. He weighs it and then looks at me. The weapon appears to be racked and the pit of my stomach tingles. This guy has no clue what he's doing. He has the pistol lying on the palm of his hand. He's tracing his silencing forefinger over the surface of the weapon: the sight, the barrel, the grip, the trigger guard, the ... The gun fires and I wince. There's a collective gasp and one of his soldiers is thrown backward against the wall as blood splatters over the cleavage of the woman's portrait behind him. The soldier slides to the floor looking more bewildered than hurt. His neck pumps blood over his coat, forming a pool on the floorboards. Gallie lopes toward the general's victim and puts the palm of her hand flat on his neck, attempting to staunch the flow. The general has thrown the gun to the ground and the facade of calm has evaporated.

"Get the physician," he barks at the officer who had handed him the pistol. After a few seconds, Gallie stands up and shakes her head.

"Not your fault," Asmus says, wearing a sympathetic expression. "Very sensitive trigger. You're not used to it, General. You and your men need training." Penrose seems to be in shock and Asmus takes advantage of it. "That pistol can fire a hundred shots a minute. Can you imagine the military advantage of having weapons like those? What's the firing rate for a flintlock musket? Three or four shots a minute? And we have guns far more–"

"Shut up," one of the officers roars and he points around the room. "Take zeez these people away."

FORTY-NINE

I fear we're being taken to the barn, but it's in the library that we end up—the one with bookshelves to the ceiling and no books. Gallie, Zhivov, Asmus and I are left looking at the door as it shuts behind us. I grab Gallie and hold her tight against me.

"Thank you," she says. "Thank you both." Zhivov shrugs. "But coming here now was a little crazed."

I turn to Asmus. "Can you think of one reason I shouldn't pummel your saggy face into pulp?" He smirks.

"Oh Joad, you know you wouldn't do that to a frail codger like myself. What would Ms. Galois think of you?" He sinks into a plush Queen Anne chair. "And by the way, I really do want to thank you for ridding me of that monstrous whore. I can't believe you stuck with her for ... how long was it? Ten years? What an appalling timeline that must have been for you. In ten years she could have courted most of Risley. And you never noticed?"

Gallie is looking at me and shakes her head. "One. You're a sad, delusional asswipe," Zhivov says. "And two, is this really what you want to talk about now?"

Asmus shrugs. "You're quite right, Dr. Zhivov. Let's save matters of the heart for another day."

"Looks like a few things changed since we left," I say.

"They've been here for a day," Gallie says. "They rolled in and I'm guessing they made short work of Leatown."

"The barn dwellers," I say. "Are they okay?" We look at Asmus.

"You're very sweet to care," he says and inspects his fingernails to prolong the moment. I start toward him. "They were in rude health yesterday. Who knows now?"

"Penrose already knew about the 'swift guns'," Gallie says. "I don't know how many of them this imbecile put out there, but they traced them back to here. That army was put together to take no chances."

"Well, *que sera, sera*." Asmus shrugs. "I can't get myself worked up over it. A customer is a customer. Right?"

"Of course." Zhivov says. "Why pick a side?"

"Precisely," Asmus says. "But I rather did like the idea of the British prevailing. What an ingenious touch. Still, spilled milk."

"So it's occurred to you that now the Americans are in control of this anachronistic arsenal that they're the ones likely to be prevailing?" I say.

"And the American victory may be *your* doing," Gallie says. "So you were trying to vandalize a timeline that itself only existed because of your vandalism." The smile momentarily slips from Asmus's face.

"You were an idiot then, and you're an idiot now," I say. "Do you see the reason TMA had no time for you? Why I had no time for you? It's because you're a deeply talentless prick." This is hitting its target. "You're not even an effective vandal." Asmus glares at me momentarily but then regains his composure.

"I'm getting rather tired," he says. "I'm sure it's not your company. Just not as young as I was, you know."

My enjoyment of the moment is spoiled as a thought bubbles up from my gut, through my throat, and to the top of my head. It's a thought that should have arrived sooner, but I had been wasting my time taunting Asmus. The

S. D. Unwin

thought is this: An air-to-surface missile armed with a massive warhead is about to bring about yet another reversal. And evaporate us in the bargain. Is the American seizure of the winning arsenal to be unceremoniously terminated and replaced by a deep, smoldering crater? And it'll be *our* doing. TMA's doing. Are we turning the Revolutionary War into a tennis match, with an inevitability of outcome bouncing back and forth, one racket held by a lunatic, the other by hapless meddlers?

Soldiers lead us up the grand staircase. We walk the hallway until one of the guards opens a door and beckons Asmus and Gallie to enter. It's a bedroom.

"No," Gallie says in unison with me and Zhivov. "I'll go with them." She points at us. The two bluecoats seem bemused.

"I was going to suggest the same thing myself," Asmus says. "Last night was such a disappointment."

"Prick," I whisper as the door is closed behind him. We walk on and a second door is opened. Before entering I turn to the guard. "There's a barn out there. Are the people in it okay? Unharmed?" The guard looks nonplussed.

"Don't know about that."

"Tell the general we need to see the people in the barn. They're innocent and have nothing to do with Asmus." He seems to digest this and then nods impatiently for us to enter.

FIFTY

Zhivov makes for the window and draws back the heavy, velvet drapes. "That's one hell of an army." We join him. Camp fires cover the terrain, diminishing to points of light in the distance, and a bright, full moon gives an iridescent quality to the landscape of white tents.

"We targeted our arrival at three days before the strike," I say to Gallie.

"You hit your mark," she replies. "Assuming the missile accel hit *its* mark, which may be a big assumption given the last-minute screw up." I sit on the corner of the bed and only then notice that it's the only bed. Is this awkward? After all, I've had sex with Gallie more than once in the corner of a barn loft not ten feet from TMAers chewing on rancid apples. Okay, am I really thinking about this now? I can't be. Maybe I can send Zhivov to check on Asmus. The guards seemed quite reasonable. Or–. "You look very pensive," Gallie says.

"Do I?" I ask. "Did Asmus–"

"He was a charming host. Gave me full run of the house as long as I didn't leave it. Then the Continental Army showed up."

"Do you hate when that happens? Fucking Continental

Army."

Zhivov lets the drape fall and throws himself into a winged chair. "We should have beat the crap out of Asmus. Then if nothing else, we would have done that."

"You know, time vandalism is easy," I say. "And then clowns like us think we can fix it and what we're really doing is joining in."

"So just sit back?" Gallie says. "Give sick little creatures like Asmus free reign?"

"But here's the thing," I say. "How do we ever know what's *supposed* to be? What we think of as the right and good timeline is maybe just the result of a thousand random acts of vandalism. If there's one Asmus, there are hundreds. So we randomly pick a timeline we think is the true one and try to get back to it. And even if we're right, whatever right is, we don't know how to repair anything because the theories are half-assed, and we wind up making the temporal quagmire worse."

"You think it's really that bad?" Zhivov asks.

"It's bad to the degree we can't even fathom. And then Prasad and his ilk have the gall to tell me and Bess we need to go back to where we came from otherwise the timeline will be damaged. I mean, seriously? It's like worrying about a mild earache when a nuclear blast is coming at you. There *is* no true timeline—no canonical history sanctioned by God and his hoards of seraphims and cherubims. It's just a big, a big—"

"Okay, Joad," Gallie says. "I know." But I don't know what she knows: whether she's agreeing with me or just saying *there, there.*

"The more I think about it, the more I think you're right, Toad" Zhivov says. Gallie and I look at him with surprise. This is a different Boris. It makes me wonder if this timeline, whichever one it is, still takes him to the directorship of TMA. His heresies of the past few days have astonished me. "Asmus, and us too, we've lived a timeline in which the colonists won the Revolutionary War. So Asmus's version of vandalism is to change that. Yet, now it's looking like he's the *reason* they won. And now our smoldering crater may reverse all of that. Maybe."

"That's all speculation," Gallie says.

"Sure it is," I say. "But so is any other explanation of a timeline. At least it hangs together ... sort of." I slide down the wall and sit up against it. "And what does it matter in the end?"

"Why does what matter?" Gallie asks.

"Whether there's an American flag or British flag flying over us."

"But it's not that simple, is it?" Gallie says. "Do you think we might accel home and the only thing that's changed is that there's a different flag flying over TMA? A change in the timeline that big is going to have an exponentially increasing domino effect on events over two centuries. It could create a history that doesn't even produce us—you, me, anyone we know."

"Then wouldn't that mean we'd already have seen the effect of ..." Pursuit of temporal logic is futile.

"But there's the theory that timelines like to heal themselves," Zhivov says. This one has already been tried on me. "That they repair the temporal perturbations and reconverge—wind up in the same or a similar place when everything sorts itself out. It's like biological evolution. You know, like placental mammals and marsupial mammals. They split apart a couple of hundred million years ago, yet when they evolved, they converged into modern animals that are pretty close to each other. Marsupial mice, moles, wolves, you know."

"You think timelines are like marsupials?" Gallie says with a faint smile.

"It's a theory."

"So if we get home alive and they ask why we fucked the timeline, let's be sure to bring up kangaroos."

It's a long night. The question of sleeping arrangements turns out to be moot as there's no sleeping going on. Zhivov stands by the window, Gallie is sitting on the bed knees pulled up to her chin and I'm sitting up against the wall, legs splayed. I revolve through our worries and it's the turn of the warhead that's about to replace us with a crater.

"The screw up on the aircraft tachyon beam. The miss. How do you feel about that?" I ask.

"She got it second time," Gallie says. "And she seemed pretty confident."

"Yeah, but she didn't know that missing her target by just two days over a range of more than two centuries would mean the difference between—"

"No, she didn't," Zhivov says. "There's no argument for us not trying to get out of here as fast as we can." Gallie and I agree.

"And the barn-full of TMAers?" Gallie asks.

"It was never our plan to rescue them on this little outing," Zhivov says. "Prasad has that in hand. We stick to that part of his plan. For now, we just need to get ourselves out of here."

"I'm curious," Gallie says. "What *was* the plan for your little outing?"

"To bring you back," I say.

"Ah," Gallie replies. "Good plan. Meticulously thought through." Our conversation tapers off and I drift in and out of sleep. The only sounds are the heavy tick of a wall clock and the occasional call of a soldier from the camps.

I'm startled awake by a thud followed by a clatter on the other side of the door. I stand and back away. The door opens and in steps the guard. "Good morning," says Gerard Bruce. He steps out and reappears dragging the unconscious sentry by the feet.

"We wondered where you got to," I say.

"Now you know."

"How did you find us?" Zhivov asks.

"You're the talk of the town," Bruce says as he ties and gags the soldier. "The mystery men with the swift guns is all they're talking about out there. And with just two rooms in this place guarded by sentries–doesn't take Sherlock Holmes."

"The barn," Gallie says. "They put you in the barn?"

"Yeah. Everyone's the worse for wear, but surviving." Bruce says, anticipating Gallie's next question. "The army's feeding us."

"Looks like you stepped out and borrowed some clothes," I say. Bruce opens the door and scans the corridor before beckoning us to follow. He leads us into the room containing Asmus. We step over the body of a second sentry to be greeted by the wide, partially-toothed grin of Mack McEwan who's in full bluecoat regalia. He's holding Asmus by the scruff of the neck.

"My deputy," Bruce says.

"What a splendid asshole you are, Mack," I say.

"Back at ya."

Asmus looks bemused. "This is very touching, but–" he says before Mack's forehead crunches fast and hard into his nose. Asmus's legs give way and he's kept upright only by Mack's grip. Gallie gives an unconvincing look of disapproval.

"You captured the sentiment of the moment, Mack," I say. That had been a glorious sound.

"I'm guessing the house is littered with guards," Zhivov says.

"It is," Bruce confirms. "I'm thinking we escort you out."

"Risky," Gallie says. "Two guards no one recognizes escorting out their prize prisoners."

"Well, whatever we decide on, let's decide soon," Mack says. "Someone is going to show up here any second."

"Asmus," Gallie says. "Have they found your Center?" Asmus is nursing his bloodied nose but still has enough wherewithal to look at Gallie in contempt. A short, threatening shake from Mack is all it takes.

"They haven't got in. They can't without me," Asmus mutters.

"If we can get there, we can accel–" Gallie begins.

"Fuck you," is what it sounds like from Asmus although the bloodied gurgle gives it comic effect.

"Do we need him to get into it?" Bruce asks.

"Yeah. Biometric access."

"Well I can cut off his face or whatever body part we need," Mack says.

"Not sure how it works," I say, but not rejecting Mack's idea. "There's also an underground passageway that'd get us out of the building, if we can get to it."

Asmus wriggles free of Mack's grip in defiant irritation. "Look, let's talk sense here my excitable friends," he says. "This is way too much drama for the circumstances we're really in." He takes a couple of steps toward me and places a hand on my forearm. "Joad, let's talk." I look down at his hand just before everything changes.

FIFTY-ONE

I'm in a sepia hologram. We're in the same room and everyone is standing where they had stood an instant before, but they have the faded red-brown hue of an antique photograph. I turn my head and I have the sense of a thousand small adjustments rather than a fluid motion. There's a profound familiarity to this, like a *deja vu* but an overwhelmingly intense one. Everyone is frozen still. Everyone except Asmus, who removes his hand from my arm and takes a step backwards. He's grinning.

"We need to have a few words," he says, and the acoustics of his voice are close and deadened, as if spoken in a bubble.

"What have you done?" I hear myself ask, but the words seem to come from somewhere distant.

"Your curiosity excites me, Joad" he says. "The first time is a wonder." I turn in an uncountable number of minute motions to look at Gallie's face and frozen into it are the beginnings of suspicion. "Can you guess what's happening? Can you?"

"You touched me," I say feebly.

"Yes, I did. Because we must speak Joad. Just you and me. You'll understand."

"Time's frozen?"

"Yet you and I aren't frozen, are we?"

"No."

"So what do you make of that?" he asks. "Think it through, Joad. No rush. Time is not pressing. Literally." He grins. Then he waits. "Tee time and Tau time. Rings any bells?" It doesn't and I shake my head in a series of tiny adjustments. "No. You never had much of an interest in my work, did you? But now you do, I think." He seats himself and dabs his nose with a handkerchief soaked in sepia blood. "I'll start you off because I know you need it. So why should space have three dimensions to it while time has but one? Seems unfair, no?" He pauses and then grins. "And as it turns out, it's untrue, too."

"Tee time and Tau time are two time dimensions?"

"They are, Joad. Quite perpendicular to one another the way left and right are perpendicular to up and down." He holds up a small disk the size of an old-fashioned pocket watch that's smooth and without markings. "Tee time I've frozen, and it's Tau time through which you and I are now in motion."

"Tau time," I echo, dumbly.

"Yes. As you see, it lacks some refinements of Tee time: more discrete, less continuous–a quantum effect I don't have time to explain. Plays with the light spectrum a little, too. But perfectly functional. It has most of the things you'd want out of a decent time dimension."

"And that little device gets us into Tau time?"

"This? It's really no more than an accelerator. Turns out that if you can sustain a backwards accel accurately enough to precisely offset forward Tee time, then Tau time shows itself. A discovery in your future–mine, too as a matter of fact."

I try to affect irritated nonchalance at this revelation, which is impossible both because of its dizzying implications, and the fact that I'm now moving around inside those implications like a sequence of drawings being flicked to create motion. He jumps up as if suddenly inspired to action. "Come with me. I want to show you the world in Tau time."

He walks and I follow him as my suspicion is trumped by awe. We walk through a sepia version of things, along the hallway, down the staircase, navigating the frozen soldiers. We step outside into a photograph: one of a landscape dotted by tents, campfires and troops, all frozen. The sky is aflame in red, like a sunset from horizon to horizon.

"You see me as a villain, Joad," Asmus says. The acoustics of his voice are unchanged by the outdoors, as if this is the sound made when people speak within a photograph. "But what am I really doing to deserve that?"

"Well, let's start with you having fifty TMA staff trapped here."

"Ah, yes. Well, take them. Take them to wherever they want to be. Although, granted, at this moment I'm not one hundred percent in control." He opens his arms at the encamped army. "But I will be soon. That'll happen."

"And there's the matter of your vandalizing the timeline," I say.

"Oh Joad, we've had that conversation. You can't accuse someone of screwing up something that's already completely screwed. Vandalism is about destroying something good, beautiful, desirable. There's no vandalism here. Maybe if we try to change the timeline often enough, then something good will come out the other end. Play the odds enough and you might win. No?"

"And that's your strategy is it? Chimps on typewriters? Maybe the chaos will in the end produce something good?"

"Come on," Asmus says. "Let's check out the barn."

Outside, it is a frozen Ramuhalli at the well pump that's producing an image of water. We enter and but for sepia hues, the scene is familiar. Bodies strewn on hay. Knots of

TMAers in conversation. I see strands of straw immobilized in mid-air, captured in Tee time during their fall from the loft.

"See. They're all intact," Asmus says. I look around to count faces–Jenn, Chen, Bisset, Wagner–as I follow Asmus out of the back door. We walk toward the tree line. "I have a proposition for you, Joad." I see the spot where Gallie and I sat together to discuss, plot, make love. "Are you curious what it is?"

"Tell me, Kasper. What's your proposition?"

"Join me," he says. I let these words float in the deadened air between us.

"Join you."

"I know I've been impulsive at times." He nods toward the barn. "And in my quieter moments, I do consider the merits of regretting that. But I want you to look past it." I snort. "I know, I know."

"Join you in what?"

"My work."

"Your work."

"Yes."

"Of making the world a better place?"

"Of at least creating the opportunity."

"By trying out every history until there's one you approve of?" I ask.

Asmus surveys me for a moment as if deciding on the best course for his argument. "The world has no resemblance to the way you comprehend it, Joad."

"I understand, so you'll keep vandalizing it–"

"No. That's not what I mean." Asmus strokes the small, disk in his hand. "I mean the very physics of it."

"Tee time and Tau time? I'd say you've demonstrated that pretty well."

"No, no. Not even that. Just adding a dimension is neither here nor there. Not in the scheme of things. That's just one more dimension added to a list we already had. I'm talking about a grand reunderstanding of things. Do you remember something you once said to me when I was the youth and you were the sage? You said, 'the universe and its physics are imbeciles'."

"Okay. That's the sort of thing I would have said."

"Well Joad, based on your understanding of the universe, you had a sound point. The problem is ... your understanding."

Asmus leans against a tree and dabs his nose. "The big guy is quite a jackass," he says.

"You happen to be right," I reply. "But he just redeemed himself."

"So, let's call it vandalism," Asmus says. "It isn't, but we'll save that conversation. So vandalism changes the timeline: makes a different history, a different future. I know your opinion of temporal logicians, and from where you started out, it's a fair one. Idiots all." I nod in a thousand small movements. "But we've come a long way since then. Ideas emerged. Theories formed. And mostly validated. And like most ideas in temporal logic they started out with your friend the great Prasad."

"What theories?" I ask. I normally wouldn't believe a syllable that Asmus emits, but I think these are matters about which lies would be sacrilege, even to him.

"As I said, with an act of 'vandalism' the timeline changes. What that means is that the universe in its entirety snaps instantly to a new structure—a new complete history, a new complete future." I nod. "Tau time plays a role in the transition but you don't need to understand that for now." Even in the incomprehensible environment of this Tau space I see smugness on Asmus's face. "Now listen to what I'm about to say carefully. When the universe makes that instant transition, all conscious perceptions of it make the same transition."

"Meaning?"

"Meaning all memories of the past, all comprehension

of the present, and all assessments of the future line up with the new reality—in an instant. You see, you shouldn't think of the universe as a place, or even as a collection of alternative places. Think of it as an experience—as billions of experiences of anyone or anything capable of having them. Maybe that picture's not quite right, but it'll get you closer to the truth than where you are now. If there's a change to the timeline, that just means all those experiences snap to that change."

"No," I say. "That isn't true. Bess and I have different memories—different pasts. In one I was with Bess for only hours, in another, years. You know that." Then I think of the park in Risley. For me it had replaced a strip mall that had been there hours before, but for the kids playing in it, it had always been there. We had different pasts. Asmus is plain wrong.

"And how do you explain it, Joad? Why did someone else's memory snap to the new timeline while yours didn't?" Prasad had asked me that same question. I had no answer then and I don't now. "I know the answer," he says. "I've known it for a while." Asmus pauses dramatically. "You see, Joad, it's you. And it's me. And it was Mancini before the idiot got himself shot up. I knew it the moment you turned up in my humble abode."

"Knew what?"

"Well, this is one time I can't really fault you for being dumb, for not figuring it out. You are dumb, but understandably so in this case. This is the kind of thing you have to be told. You just don't have the facts. So let's take a step back ... tackychemistry ... the three magical chemicals. The little buggers that started it all."

"Go on."

"Well, this is interesting. It turns out that analogs to those chemicals, in micro quantities, are produced by human glands." He pauses. "Let that sink in, Joad." He pauses again. "Is it sinking in?"

"Yes, it's sinking in, Kasper. Consider it sunken-in. Just

tell me."

"And for some fraction of us, I'm guessing a small fraction, the chemicals are produced in just the right proportions–the Goldilocks effect. Are you ahead of me yet? You should be ahead of me." I don't give him the satisfaction of a response, and I am not ahead of him. "Those chemicals create a highly localized tachyon field."

"And–?"

"And for those lucky few, their memories are immunized against the new timeline. To the extent they snap to the new reality, their memories don't snap with them. They retain their old timeline." I look around myself, buying time to absorb this. "And when I saw you react to Elizabeth for the first time, I knew right then that you were one of us. That you remembered your life with her." I kneel down on the grass to avoid falling. "You see how important that is don't you?"

"Yes," I say without thinking.

"You can't compare histories if you don't remember them."

"No."

"And that's why I need you on my team," he says. "You know, at one time I wanted to take you and make you suffer a little along with the others. Then I wanted to kill you because you were the one that got away. I do tend to ruminate over these things; you know, whip myself up into a frenzy, and maybe I got it a little out of proportion. But then when I discovered your gift, I became a little ambivalent to be honest. So, you see, I'm just a man with human foibles–I can get confused, torn. You have to give me some slack, Joad. Anyway, I realized it would have been a monstrous shame to just kill you. And now I'm seeing what should have been obvious to me much sooner. We need to be partners, you and me."

I look up at him and there's nothing but sincerity on his jowled, sepia face, looking like an antique photograph of a long dead relative. Could there be a quark of truth to this?

To think that words emitted from Kasper Asmus could possibly be anything but lies is itself an act of insanity. Yet ... I believe him. Or at least, I think he believes himself.

"The scientist in you has only one option, Joad. You can't walk away from this offer–to learn and understand more about the nature of things in one week than in your whole mediocre career. Jump on this."

"I need to get back to the mansion," I say. The missile. I can't be here with this lunatic.

"You're worried about Galois and your little band of brothers? It's sweet that you care about such small matters." He smiles warmly. "But there are a few things I need to make happen first–things that'll leave Penrose in no doubt who's in control. Once that's all figured out, we can get your little team taken care of." Asmus reaches up and runs his finger along a leaf frozen in mid fall. "Now, are you with me, Joad Bevan?"

"What do you want from me?" I ask.

"Good question." He strokes the small accelerator disk with his thumb. "First thing, let's accel forward a couple of days. By then Penrose will be extremely anxious to talk with me and willing to accept terms quite favorable to us."

Us! I feel a pang of disgust.

"So we'll simply saunter up, in full control of the situation, and talk business."

Then my neck turns cold as what he had said catches up with me. Accel forward two days! The day of the strike, always assuming it hadn't happened before.

"No!"

"No?"

"We need to make sure Gallie, Zhivov and the others are safe. We need to get right back there, in the now."

"You're such a worrywart, Joad. That's not going to work in your new job. Believe me, your friends are going nowhere with the Continental Army guarding them. They have no chance of getting out of there." Then I see his thumb beginning to trace out patterns on the accel disk.

"Trust me."

FIFTY-TWO

Tee time has returned and I'm looking into a cloudless, blue sky. I've lost my bearings. We're on open ground and now I see the mansion ahead. But the camp has gone and there's not a soul, not a tent, not a campfire remaining. I turn back to see Asmus. He's surveying the landscape and looking confused. Then he tells me to follow him. I feel my heart thudding hard against my rib cage. I look up again to scan the sky knowing that if I were to see anything it'd be too late. I begin to run toward the mansion. Everything I care about is in it. I run faster shouting "Come on!" to no one. The mansion is a couple of hundred yards ahead of me. No sentries outside, neither goon nor soldier. I hear a distant whistle that becomes a scream in the instant it takes me to look up. Something dark passes over me at unfathomable speed and I look ahead to see the mansion become a haze of gray, orange and red. A sack of anvils swings into my chest as I feel the ground drop from beneath my feet.

Silence. Absolute silence. I open my eyes to dense, swirling points of light that slowly part to reveal patterns of shifting black and blue. My heart pounds soundlessly. I focus enough to see thick black smoke passing over me in waves. I try to move but feel white hot bolts being driven into my ribs. I take a breath, grit my teeth and push myself up onto my elbows. Ahead, there's no vestige of a building or of any structure: just flames and billowing smoke. I grit my teeth hard and look toward the barn. Two walls remain standing. No movement, no sign of life. Is this how I go? I would never have guessed it.

It's a wonderfully silly ending.

I see movement near the barn and squint at it. A horse mounted by a bluecoat emerges from the tree line. Then another, and then around them, foot soldiers walking out tentatively without formation. There are tens, then hundreds of them emerging. From between the soldiers bursts a figure running directly toward me. As the figure gets closer I whisper "Gallie." My elbows give way and with an unbearable jolt of pain I'm on my back again. No time seems to pass, or maybe I lost consciousness, but now she's kneeling by me, her face above mine and her hair touching my cheek. She's mouthing words I can't make out and I smile. Then I see Zhivov above her grinning down at me. "Such a pinhead, Toad," is what he mouths. I stare up at him and then blackness comes in from the edges.

FIFTY-THREE

I'm not dead is my first thought. My field of view is white. I feel my hand being squeezed and I move my eyes from the white to see Gallie.

"What?" is the thing I say and I wince with the effort it took. She smiles at me.

"What?" she repeats. "You're okay. Banged up, but okay." I swallow and even that hurts. "You're bruised with a few cracked ribs. That's all." I look down to see bandages wrapped around my chest.

"You got out in time," I whisper.

Gallie nods. "General Penrose is a reasonable man it turns out. He went along with the possibility of something very nasty coming from the sky."

"My TMAers?"

"All intact. Worse for wear most of them, but alive."

"The barn—"

"Yes, I'd say Prasad was off in his calculations. But we'd gotten them out of there." I turn my head toward Gallie and wince.

"The arsenal?"

"The missile hit its target spot on. Gone. Don't know about Asmus."

"We acceled here just before the hit. He was alive then." Talking hurts.

"We didn't see him."

I hazard a few shallow breaths. At least the arsenal is gone. But Asmus is at large. How big a problem is that? Would he really bother to go through all of that again? To rebuild his empire of barking madness? Maybe he's old enough to settle down to just having unhinged thoughts by a roaring fire. Maybe.

"So we can go?" I ask. "Go home?"

"Not broached that with the general yet, but he's being a charming host," Gallie says.

For the first time, I scan my surroundings. I see TMAers looking back at me. Jenn, Mack, Ramuhalli, and others too far away to get in focus. "When Prasad comes in," I whisper, "he won't find what he expected. What's ..." I lose my question and the weight of my eyelids shuts me down again.

I count two days and two nights, and with each the pain diminishes provided I avoid any rapid movement. I can sit up, and along with everyone else in the TMA marquee, I speculate on the timing and tactics of our rescue. I share with Gallie and Zhivov my conversation with Asmus, or most of it, and we agree to analyze it later. There are different priorities for now. Unlike the others in this tent, for me going home is no matter for elation. A few cracked ribs will heal soon enough, but the prospect of being sent to a home a-quarter-of-a-century from Gallie is the real agony.

On the third day I hear a commotion outside the tent along with soldiers barking orders at each other. The tent flap is lifted and in ducks Penrose. He doesn't have an entourage but just one soldier who waits by the flap. Penrose approaches me, tall and formidable in his blue and gold.

"Are you feeling better Mr. Bevan?" he asks.

I look at Gallie and Zhivov. "I am, General. Thank you."
He nods his acknowledgment.

"I wish for you to meet some people," he says, and turns
to signal the soldier who then lifts the tent flap. A man
enters, then a woman, another woman and another man.
They're in eighteenth century attire but their bulky
backpacks are not contemporary. Hushed conversations
break out. Gallie, Zhivov and I exchange panicked looks.
They've captured the rescue team. Penrose studies me. "I
believe these are your colleagues here to take you home." I
stare at him, then at each of the rescue team, ideas for escape
shooting through my brain as if I had the strength to make
any of them happen. "I shall leave you to do your work," he
says. He's about to turn when Zhivov speaks up.

"Thank you General," he says. Penrose nods slowly,
turns and walks toward the flap. But then he stops and looks
back. "You should be where you belong with the things that
belong to you. And we should be where we belong with the
things that belong to us. This is the natural way."

Knowing that all of this mess was the doing of nature
did not tempt me to contradict him.

"General," I say on an impulse. "Are you going to win
this thing?" He stares at me for a moment until a brief smile
of comprehension crosses his face.

"I do believe we shall prevail, Mr. Bevan. I do."

The backpacks are full of wrist accelerators. The
marquee billows in the wind as if with laughter, disbelief,
and joy. In ones and twos we pop and the sounds of excited
conversation taper out. Prasad had the devices preset and
my team accel to 2021. That's what the immutable laws of
TMA had dictated, and what Prasad demanded. They're set
to arrive shortly after the destruction of the array.

"I'm sure they'll pick up the pieces," Gallie says.

"They've got the leadership to help them through it," I
say, looking at Boris. He agrees without a hint of

cognizance. He really doesn't know. Zhivov, Gallie and I are the last to be handed our accelerators. I tap mine to display the destination. *1996.* I exhale and smile. Gallie is watching me.

"Prasad needs your debrief, Joad," she says dolefully. "That's all."

"One day at a time, Gallie. Prasad can have his *one second per second*, but you gotta let me be happy one day at a time."

FIFTY-FOUR

A few days in hospital got me on my feet again. I was declared free of blast lung, eye rupture and brain injury, which came as little relief because I hadn't been informed enough to worry. Prasad and Abioye had no patience for a written report and spent several hours a day in my hospital room, Prasad using two fingers to prod my words into his chunky laptop. I gave them the whole story, at least as much as I could remember, but for one exception: Asmus's theory that I was special–a manufacturer of magical chemicals. That didn't make it into Prasad's laptop. I hadn't told Gallie or Boris either. I'm not sure why I held this back, but it seemed like sharing it would be nothing but trouble. Maybe the time would come, but I was just not in the mood for it.

It was during a visit from Boris that I learned Bess had escaped. This made me smile. She had told me she'd be fucked if Prasad would send her back to her twenty-first century misery, and it turned out he didn't and she wasn't. I was a little surprised by it but then I was surprised at my surprise. This is Bess, after all. I asked Boris how she could have escaped and he reminded me that she was being kept at the TMA site, not San Quentin. Stealing keys and driving away didn't take a Houdini.

ONE SECOND PER SECOND

And Gallie was with me when the others were not. We said little. There was little need. We spent time watching the TV together in my hospital room, or her telling me about acceleration detection events of the day. I even learned how to express credible interest in her cat's health. With that, I had Zhivov at a disadvantage.

I returned to TMA and Prasad informed me of my departure date. He thought it better not to linger. The next day I'd be in the place TMA has deemed my home, and the rules were immutable: that's where I'd be going.

I awake to see Gallie looking up at me. Her head is on my shoulder and her arm draped across my chest.

"Good morning," she whispers. But it really isn't.

"Hi."

We're squeezed into the cot designed to barely accommodate one adult, but the fit feels warm and comfortable. "We can do it, you know. We can do what Bess did. Get in a car and we're gone." Gallie sighs.

"You're no Bess. And neither am I."

"No." We lie quietly. "Do you think it's really as screwed up as we think? As Asmus says it is?" She seems to be pondering it.

"I don't know, Joad. I suppose he would say that. Maybe it is, maybe it's not." She strokes my chest. I should want to make love but my thoughts are too heavy. I kiss her forehead and sit up.

"It feels like I'm going to the gallows. But without having my favorite meal first."

"Is your favorite meal a muffin?" Gallie asks.

"Yes!" I say in a *how did you know?* voice.

"Then I have a silver lining for you," she says, clambering over me to get down from the cot.

We meet with Boris, Prasad and Abioye in the

conference room. There's no chatter. Everyone knows what they're about to do to me, and to Gallie. And they know we accept it. I'm handed a wrist accelerator and I put it on. Prasad had at least allowed me to pick my arrival point and I'd chosen the place on the Columbia River bank from where I'd first set out. The accelerator had been programmed to return here after I'd removed it.

I don't hold Gallie, not here. I'm not that strong.

"We'll meet again, Toad," I hear Boris say. He's right.

Then I'm bathed in bright sunlight and a chilled breeze hits me.

FIFTY-FIVE

The thought of returning to the dank and dismal place my home had become was too dispiriting and so I had checked into a hotel on the riverfront. From my window, I watch the kayaks and power boats go by, the children playing on the grassy banks, and couples strolling or cycling by together. In the evenings I walk out onto the pier behind the hotel and watch the darkening sky. A few miles north of here is the TMA site which I'm sure is in the process of being rebuilt, but I have no appetite for being there. Not yet. I receive phone calls from my TMA friends: my barnmates. Some sound as they always have. Some are changed.

We'd made an agreement, Gallie and I. It was an agreement to something neither of us really had the power to ensure. I would take a month to reach the right decision. A month to catch my breath in the place I'm from, to weigh up the bizarre circumstances, and then to do the proper thing. I agreed to the month. After all, for Gallie it was twenty five years, so it was the least I could do. I didn't need the month. I didn't need an hour. And the days passed sluggishly.

It's the morning of the day. I'm early and I pace slowly around the path that follows the perimeter of the small park—my magical park that never was. I'd paced it a dozen times over the previous month as if to practice for today. I see a group of little kids chasing each other around the central rectangle as their parents watch on, laugh and chat. In the center of the rectangle is a pale, basalt column. To pass time I cross the grass and walk up to it. It's about two feet in diameter and ten feet tall. On it I notice a bronze plaque and I read it.

This park is dedicated to Dave and Bess Levinsky whose generous support of the City of Risley Park Foundation has made possible this and other places of beauty.

I look away, take a breath and then read it again. I smile. "It wouldn't surprise me," I whisper to myself. "No one has given me more surprises than you." I read it one last time and then turn to walk back toward the path.

It's then that I see her. It's her, unmistakably. She's standing by a park bench and she's looking at me. My pace quickens to a jog, and then a sprint. I grab Gallie and hold her to me. Then I pull back to look into her face. It's a face that I see aged by my single month apart from her rather than by the years she must have counted. The second kiss lasts longer—much longer.

"I was terrified you wouldn't come," I say. She smiles and strokes my cheek.

"So was I—that *you* wouldn't." We sit down on the bench together, eyes locked, holding hands.

"Don't tell me anything yet, I just want to look at you."

"Okay," she whispers. "Can I tell you just one thing?" She looks away from me and I realize after a few moments that she's looking at the man approaching us. *Oh no. No, no.* It's the husband of twenty years. But as he approaches, I see he's a young man in no more than his twenties. He's slender and his gait is graceful and fluid. His light brown hair is drawn up into a bun on the crown of his head and his eyes are blue and sharp. I look at Gallie in surprise and then stand to be introduced. He holds out his hand and I grasp it. I look into his eyes. They're the eyes in my mirror. And no introduction is needed.

"Gallie," I whisper. She stands.

"Are you okay?" she asks. I look at her, then back at this young guy.

"Come on, let's go" she says and the three of us walk toward the park gate.

"Any other surprises for me?" I ask as we follow our son along the path.

"No," she says. "Oh, the cat died."

"That's sad," I say, and we begin to catch up, one second per second.

ABOUT THE AUTHOR

S. D. Unwin started out as a theoretical physicist searching for the Holy Grail of a quantum theory of gravity. He later turned his mathematical skills to analyzing and communicating catastrophic risk, from nuclear mishaps to climate change. *One Second Per Second* is his first science fiction novel. He lives on Bainbridge Island in Puget Sound.

SDUnwin.com

ALSO BY S. D. UNWIN

FALL OF TIME
The sequel to One Second Per Second

THE MAGNI

Printed in Great Britain
by Amazon